DESTINED FOR THE FAE KING

MATED TO THE FAE KING BOOK TWO

BAILEY DARK

Copyright © 2019 by Bailey Dark

All rights reserved.

No part of this book may be reproduced in any form or by any electronic or mechanical means, including information storage and retrieval systems, without written permission from the author, except for the use of brief quotations in a book review.

BLURB

"She shivers as I drag my tongue across her jugular. It's been too long since I kissed this woman. Too long since I felt her heat in my arms. She writhes against me, panting, and I grin ferally. "

Verity Chastain almost died saving her sadistic, charming kidnapper from the curse that threatened to take his life and destroy his kingdom. But something awoke inside her when she broke his curse, something dark.

Struggling to discover her past and her future, Verity pulls away from the one man who could save her. With their relationship fraying at the seams, Altair is desperate to find a way to save his kingdom from the Bloodbane witches. When news arrives that the Bloodbane are preparing to start a war, Altair's desperation reaches new heights.

Dark forces are brewing on Alnembra's borders, as they are in Verity's heart.

CHAPTER 1

The healer bends over my belly, his lips pursed as they study what's left of the stab wound. I wince as he prods the laceration delicately; even the smallest touches send the pain flaring. He murmurs to himself and then withdraws a salve from his robes. It smells pungent, like ginger or mustard. I wrinkle my nose as he swipes the yellow cream over the gash in my belly.

Almost every day the healers have a new cream to apply to aid in the healing process. They seem almost baffled that I haven't healed completely yet after two weeks. But I'm human, not Fae. I clamber to my feet and lift my arms so the healer can wrap a bandage around my belly. His fingers are cool and nimble, like little kisses of snow against my skin.

When he's finished, I tug my shirt back down over my belly. He passes me the cane with a smile. "Many blessings, Curse-Breaker," he says bowing.

I force a smile. "Many blessings."

Curse-Breaker. That's what the servants and healers have been calling me in whispered breaths. No one saw what happened between Altair, Maaz, and I. No one knows that breaking the curse was as simple as pledging my life to his – whatever that means. I inhale sharply, staring into empty space. I know what it means. I know what it meant.

I swallow thickly. My engagement to Henry ended in such a mess I'm in no hurry to be engaged again. And yet here I am – sworn to a Fae King. The cane is a heavy weight in my hands as I force myself to lean on it and leave the healer's chambers. I do my best to stand tall while supporting myself on the cane, but in the end, I look like a hunched old woman.

I pass halls filled with smiling servants and stoic guards. They bow or curtsy as I pass before returning to their duties. I don't think I'll ever get used to the strange obeisance they show me. I'm not a Curse-Breaker or a hero, I'm just a girl. Altair hasn't noticed any difference in the Fae's behavior, but he's kept busy running his country for the first time in a thousand years.

I bite my lip as I think of him; the man I swore myself to. He hasn't pressed me for marriage yet, but I can only assume that's because of my injury. I almost don't want the gash to heal if it can put off my future. My uncertain future. With the wound, I know what happens day in and day out.

Breakfast. Reading. Lunch. Healers. Dinner. A short visit from Altair. Sleep.

The days are boring and drag on, but I know at the end of them I won't be pressed for decisions. There's too much for me to think about. Too many questions. And right now, the only question on my mind, the only one that constantly plagues me, is who I am. What I am. I slow as I approach the library. The halls are always emptier around the library, I don't feel so rushed to make my way out of the eyes of the servants and guards.

Altair and others insist that the Bloodbane oath flows through my veins. I know it's true. I felt it when the witches kidnapped me and held me so tightly. I felt it when I said the words that ended Altair's curse. I feel it now. My Bloodbane ancestry is like lead in my veins. I feel it always, a constant pressure. It's a reminder of what abilities and powers lie in store for me. Even that is a mystery. Altair refuses my questions about the Bloodbane, my requests to know my own history. I grimace, my past and future feels lost to me.

At the door of the library I pause and catch my breath. Walking long distances, even from one end of the palace to the other, often leaves me short of breath now. I come to the library almost every day searching for answers or clues as to who I am and what my covenant with Altair means.

This world of magic, Fae, and witches is new to me. New and unfamiliar. And wholly different from anything I expected when I imagined these fantastical realms before. There is only one thing about myself and my blood I'm certain of. The Bloodbane witches gain their power from their binding to Sadal Malik. They wed him figuratively and he gives them their power. He would have given me my power if I had said my oath to him and not Altair.

I don't know what happens to me now that I'll be binding myself to another man and not the Dark God. Another question no one has been able to answer. Perhaps I won't have access to powerful magic anymore. Maybe nothing will change at all. After all, Altair isn't an ancient god. But ever since I said the words, the oath in my veins has been singing constantly. Waiting for something. Or someone.

I shake my head, trying to clear my mind of the anxiety I feel almost constantly now. I head to the far corner of the library, where the tomes on magic and the Bloodbane witches are kept. With the cane in one hand, and two heavy texts in the other, I waddle back to the center of the room to a chair pushed up beside the window.

With a grunt, I heave the books onto an adjacent table and settle carefully into the chair. Sunshine pours through the windows, warming my chilled skin. I open the first book and flip to the first page. It's a history of the Bloodbane witch clans.

There are five in total, with many divisions within the major clans. They have a complex structure of leadership. But their Chieftess is always the strongest among them. Maaz.

I feel a tingle of fear trickle down my spine as I think of her. She's ancient; several thousand years old. And she's led the Bloodbane witches for most of them. I remember her cruel, blue eyes as she glowered at me during our last encounter. She was murderous and frightening. The memory of her blade burying itself in my belly after she threw it towards Altair sends my heart racing. I'm breathing too quickly, too shallowly. I clutch the arm rests beside me, digging my nails into the soft velvet.

Panic floods through me and it's as if I'm back in that moment when I thought my life was ending. The pain in my belly flares as my blood pumps faster. I know it's slipping through the stitches now and beginning to soak the bandage. I clench my eyes shut, forcing myself to take deep breaths.

I lurch as I feel a strong hand on my shoulder. "It's okay, Verity, you're safe," Altair murmurs.

My eyes open enough to see him crouch in front of me. He presses his hands on my legs, attempting to ground me. "Altair," I whisper fearfully.

"Shh." His brows are furrowed. "Breathe."

After a few moments of struggling to catch my breath, I feel my heart settle. I inhale deeply and then release the breath slowly. My muscles relax, and I can finally open my eyes completely. "I'm sorry," I say as I stare into his hazel eyes.

His black hair is swept back, revealing the tips of his pointed ears. His full lips are pulled into a concerned smile. My eyes rake over his frame. Even crouched before me, it's obvious that he's tall and lean. His tunic is unlaced near the collar, just enough to reveal a slip of hair.

"You have nothing to be sorry for," he says. I nod. Altair takes the book from my lap and inspects it. "Just a bit of light reading?"

I blanch, knowing what he thinks of me learning about the

Bloodbane. "I know it's dangerous to involve myself with Blood-bane magic, but it's part of who I am. And since the curse was broken, I've felt so lost," I say softly.

"What do you mean?" He frowns.

I bite my lip. "Whether you or I like it, I am a Bloodbane. At least, almost. But now that I've made my vow to you and not to Sadal Melik, I don't know what happens next. I don't know what happens to me and my magic."

"It's a little early in your life to be having an existential crisis," he says, cocking a brow.

"Altair." I glower at him.

He laughs softly. "I know." His eyes grow serious and his voice lowers. "You're Verity Chastain, you're the Curse-Breaker. And my future wife."

My heart beats wildly at his words. Curse-Breaker. Wife. "That's a lot to put on a librarian's shoulders," I whisper. My gut is twisted and heavy.

"You've been cooped up in this castle for too long," Altair quips, rising. "Let me take you to see Desmarais, the City of Glass."

I furrow my brows and sink back into the chair. "Is it safe?"

"You don't have to worry, Verity," Altair says gently. "Maaz and her witches are far from Desmarais."

"I can hardly walk." I tilt my chin towards the cane next to me. "I barely made it from the healer's tower to the library."

"Not to worry; I'll take you on a grand tour in my carriage," Altair says.

I purse my lips but rise shakily to my feet. I am eager to get out of the palace and the palace grounds. The palace is all I've seen of Altair's kingdom, except the wilderness from my last abduction. I reach for my cane, grimacing in pain, but excitement tugs at my heart. I feel lighter already.

"Is it really that terrible?" He asks, cocking a brow.

"I feel like an old woman," I sigh.

Suddenly, Altair's strong arms sweep me off my feet. He lifts me into the air easily and holds me against his chest. My eyes widen and I gasp softly at the sudden move. My cane clatters to the floor, the sound echoing through the empty library. Altair's eyes rove over me, a smile playing at his lips. An image of the two of us pressed together, lips trailing kisses over bare skin, flits through my mind. My cheeks heat at the thought, but I can't tear my gaze away from his full lips.

"I can walk on my own," I say, wiggling in his arms.

A soft purr rumbles from his chest. "I can't let a woman as beautiful as you suffer."

"Altair," I say, my voice carrying a hint of a whine.

"Do you want me to drop you?" He cocks a brow.

I yelp as he relaxes his arms long enough to let me slip a few inches closer to the ground. "You are such a bastard," I hiss, clinging to his chest.

Altair chuckles low, adjusting his grip. His hand grazes my ass and my breath hitches in my throat. "If that's what I have to be for the pleasure of feeling you in my arms," he purrs. I go stiff, a blush creeping to my cheeks. "Do you know it's been weeks since I last held you close?"

"No," I stammer. I've kept Altair at a distance since the night I broke his curse.

"Liar," he murmurs. "Let me hold you like this."

We fall silent as he strides out of the library. I relax into his arms as he sweeps out the main door and down the castle steps to the awaiting carriage. I bite my lip as he sets me down gently in front of the door. I climb onto the first step, hands on the door frame to hoist myself in. I can feel Altair's eyes on me and it sends a thrill coursing through me.

There's a loud clatter and I turn instinctively to find the source of the noise. My heart beats out of time in my chest as I make eye contact with a Fae gardener. His eyes are a deep brown, black from a distance, and his skin is pale like ivory. He's tall, with a lithe figure. His lips are quirked into a wicked smile as I meet his gaze. He turns away to pick up his fallen tools and I can't help but stare at his lean muscles. It feels as if time itself has frozen in that instant, everything falls away except the gardener's eyes.

Behind me, Altair gently nudges one of my hands free, as if to assist me. I blink, drawing my gaze away from the beautiful Fae. With Altair's help, I clamber into the carriage and settle in the corner. The cushions of the carriage seats are a plush, red velvet with gold trim. He slams the door as he sits. The carriage is large enough to fit Altair's large frame and then some.

We trundle away from the palace as I quell the excitement in my chest. Altair smiles at me from across the carriage; a patient, hopeful smile. I meet his gaze, chewing on my bottom lip. I'm not used to the thoughtful and kind version of Altair that he's projecting today. I turn away, pretending to stare at the palace grounds as we approach the gates. I imagine I see the gardener again, this time in the shade of a mulberry tree. I drag my gaze away from the tricky shadows and peek at Altair from behind a sheet of my brown hair.

He seems so at relaxed now that the curse is broken, and his country is his again. He's fallen back into his duties without any trouble, and I know it makes him happy to be working again. Be stagnant for so long should have driven him mad. He lounges back in the chair, comfortable in the silence between us. I should be happy for him. But my own questions and doubts are always lingering in the back of my mind, like a cobweb in the corner.

CHAPTER 2

ALTAIR

Verity is warm in my arms as I carry through the castle halls. Her petite frame has grown even lighter in the past weeks since she's been injured. I hide a frown, wondering if she's eating well enough. I should be eating with her and spending more time with her, but my duties as King keep me away for most hours of the day.

I hold her a little closer, wishing again that she hadn't jumped in front of the blade for me. It shocked me then, and I still haven't been able to fully understand why she did it. Verity and I keep each other at arm's length despite what we've been through together. The only thing that brings me hope that she might feel as strongly for me as I do for her is that she sacrificed herself for me. She's settled in my arms, but her lips are twisted into an expression of discomfort. I suppose after losing so much precious time to be with her, it's only natural that we've lost the familiarity between us.

I don't know that I would even kiss her the way I used to. My heart clenches in my chest. Verity is to be my wife. I can't let this distance continue. It's too much already, a small rift between us where we should only be knitted closer together. She peeks up at me with her pale blue eyes and I grin at her. I'll pretend I'm not worried. I'll pretend that we're alright.

Outside, the sun is still high in the sky. It warms my skin and I smile more broadly. Only a few weeks ago, I hadn't felt the sun on my bare skin in a thousand years. I missed its warm glow. No one could possibly understand just how much I cherish being in my Fae form in broad daylight now. It's a gift.

The carriage is waiting outside and I set Verity in front of it gently. She pauses and stares into the distance, her hands on the doorframe. I trail a finger down her back and follow her gaze. There's a gardener collecting some fallen tools. He and Verity lock eyes before he glances sharply at me. I curl my lip at him on reflex, my more territorial Fae nature revealing itself. I nudge Verity forward, drawing her attention away from the handsome gardener. She moves sluggishly, as if waking from a dream.

I follow her into the carriage and draw the curtains on my side so the gardener is hidden from view. But Verity seems to have forgotten about him now; she stares out her own window at the familiar gardens.

I watch her carefully as she gazes out the window. The carriage rolls forward, following the long drive to the castle walls. She shrinks back into the cushions, covering her face with her long brown hair. I smile, pleased that Verity and I can finally enjoy time together. For the past two weeks, after the healers determined that she wasn't going to die, I've only been able to find a few minutes to spend with her. I drop my gaze as guilt tugs at my heart. I should find more time to spend with her.

She clears her throat. "Don't you have more to do as King?"

"I cancelled all of my appointments today," I explain, sliding across the bench so I'm directly across from her.

"Can you do that?" She looks surprised.

I place a hand on her knee and squeeze lightly. "The country was stagnant for a thousand years; it can be stagnant for another day."

Verity blushes softly and falls silent as we pass through the castle gates. The road to Desmarais is a decline, lined with tall trees and lamplights. There are a few wagons trundling down the road, returning from bringing goods to the castle. Verity leans forward, her face halfway out the window so she can take it all in. I feel a pang of regret that this is the first time verity has been out of the castle walls with permission. She was trapped like a little bird for so long. But there was no helping it; the Bloodbane witches would have killed her otherwise.

The wagons pull off the road to allow us to pass, they recognize the royal sigil on the doors. The castle slowly disappears above us, perched on a cliff that overlooks the city. Verity peers up at it, taking in the buttresses and elegant towers.

"Verity," I say softly as the scent of delicate spices reaches my nose. She turns at the sound of my voice and her eyes widen as she notices the sight laid out before her. "Welcome to Desmarais, the City of Glass."

Her lips are parted softly as we enter the outskirts of the city. The City of Glass is not named so because of its architecture or building materials, but rather because of the bright and pearlescent light that shines in the night and day. It glows merrily with lamplight that reflects off of the white stucco of the buildings. Verity's hands clutch the windowsill as she stares at the crowds of Fae wandering through the shopping streets. The road is lined with buildings packed side by side with large windows displaying baked goods, jewels, clothes, and more. Fae children dart between the carriages that wander down the road. She gasps at the sight of them and points.

I laugh. "Yes, there are children."

"How old?" She asks, her voice breathless with delight.

I peek out the window and squint at the children. "I would guess maybe seventy-five years old."

"Seventy-five," she echoes. She bursts into bright laughter and my heart warms at the sound. "They're older than me."

"It's been a long time since I heard you laugh," I murmur.

She glances at me, startled, and then bites her lip. "It's been a long time since I've laughed at all."

Wordlessly, I move across the carriage to sit beside her. She edges closer to the wall, away from me, pain lances through my chest but I try to ignore the subtle distance. I lean over her and point out the window, showing her the different sights of Desmarais.

"What's that?" Verity asks, pointing to a tall, white spire in the distance.

"That's the Library of Desmarais," I say. "It has the greatest collection of knowledge in the world."

"I thought your private library was impressive," she whistles softly. "I'd love to see it."

I smile. A visit to the library would be perfect for Verity. "Perhaps another day, they aren't open to the public. Even I have to arrange a visit beforehand."

"But you're the King," she says incredulously.

"Yes, but they're the librarians." I grin, nudging her shoulder gently. I peek out the window in time to see the window display of a famous jeweler in Desmarais. "Driver, stop here please."

The carriage rolls to a stop and Verity looks around, worry bunching her brows. "What are you doing?"

"I wanted to visit one of my favorite stores," I say, opening the door and crawling around her. I hop out of the carriage and onto the cobblestones. Verity bites her lip but takes my outstretched hand to leave the carriage.

"Is it alright for you to walk around like this? Out in the open?" She asks softly as the crowds of Fae go quiet.

They stare as we stride past. I lean close to her ear and when I speak, she shivers pleasantly. "Fae don't bite. Except on occasion," I tease her.

She purses her lips, glaring at me for a moment before suddenly lurching to the side. Panic flares in my belly as Verity presses herself into me, a soft whimper escaping her lips. I turn furious eyes on the Fae who startled her. But it's only an elderly Fae woman draped in a light shawl. I resist the urge to bare my teeth and, instead, only throw a protective arm around Verity.

"I'm sorry, Your Grace," the woman says in a lilting voice. "I didn't mean to startle her. I only wanted to thank the Curse-Breaker."

Verity stiffens at the name. I run my thumb over her arm to soothe her. "Lady Chastain," I say to the Fae. "You may call her Lady Chastain."

"Lady Chastain, you have my gratitude." The woman's voice trembles.

Verity nods. "It was nothing," she stammers.

Without another word, I lead Verity away from the Fae woman. Slowly, the Fae turn their attention away from us, having gotten their fill of the King and his Curse-Breaker. Verity detaches herself from me, wincing as pain lances through her belly. I glance back at the carriage, where her cane is tucked away.

"I'll get your cane," I say, turning away partially.

She latches onto my arm. "No," she says firmly. "I'm fine."

"Verity," I murmur.

"Show me the store, I want to see." She turns away from the carriage stubbornly.

I take her arm and show her to a jeweler renowned for his detail and artistry. The white of Desmarais is practically glowing under the sun. The glass windows of the shop glitter brilliantly as the sun strikes the jewels on display.

She blanches nervously at the decadent jewelry in the windows, but I push through the blue door and bring her into the elegant shop. The jeweler, a Fae man named Tinle, scurries from the back. His eyes widen as he takes me in. I extend a hand to him, grinning.

"Tinle, it's been a long time," I say warmly.

He bows before accepting my outstretched hand. "Your Grace, you do me a great honor."

"Tinle, I'd like you to meet Verity Chastain. Verity, this is the world's greatest jewel artist," I say.

Tinle scoffs in forced humility but doesn't deny my words. Verity dips her chin. "It's a pleasure to meet you."

"And you," Tinle says, his keen eyes roving over her. "What can I do for you, Your Grace?"

"I'm looking for something unique, something one of a kind for Verity," I say, following him to one of his display cases.

Tinle nods understandingly and disappears into the back. Verity tugs at my sleeve. "What are you doing?" She hisses under her breath.

"Buying you a gift." I smile, knowing that she'll only continue to protest.

"You don't have to," she says, a strain to her voice.

"I want to," I say firmly. I meet her gaze and squeeze her hand. "Let me, it's for my own benefit really. You would be doing me a favor."

She purses her lips. "Alright, but nothing too expensive."

"Verity," I murmur, leaning closer to her. "I have a thousand years of unspent gold, a thousand years of savings. I could buy you the world."

She gapes as Tinle returns, carrying a small silver box. He lays it gently on the display case and opens it with reverence. My lips part as I take in the delicate silver chain, studded with precious gems the color of my eyes.

Tinle grins, obviously pleased at my reaction. "It's amber," he says proudly.

"Fossilized tree sap?" Verity cocks a brow.

Tinle bristles. "Not just any amber. These particular stones were cut from amber found along the banks of the elusive Motabilem River."

I loose a breath, impressed. "And how were they acquired?"

"By an agent of mine many centuries ago. I've kept them locked up tight until the right buyer came along," Tinle explains.

"I don't understand." Verity glances between the two of us. "Why does this river make the amber more precious?"

"It's a moving river," I say.

"All rivers move," she says pointedly.

I chuckle. "No, the river is never in the same place. One day it could be deep in the mountains beyond our border, and the next, it could be south, pouring into the Azul sea. It might spend weeks in the Nubes Forest and then two days in Meridianam."

Her brows furrow. "How is it possible?"

I shrug. "No one knows."

Tinle straightens his shoulders. "As you can see, the gems are very precious."

"But how do we know they truly are from the Mo-," she trails off and then purses her lips. "This river?"

"Verity," I murmur. "Tinle is a man of great integrity."

Tinle lifts the necklace and hands Verity a delicate magnifying glass. "Look at the gem." He waits for her to peer at the stone. "Do you see the swirls of white in the gem? It's subtle, difficult to see."

"I see it," Verity says.

"The Motabilem River is unique in that its waters carry a strange liquid, which we can only assume is related to the magical way the river appears wherever it likes." Tinle drapes the necklace back in the box. "The presence of that material in the amber itself is an indication that it was taken from the banks of the Motabilem River."

Verity bites her lip. "I see. I meant no offense."

"It's alright," Tinle says. "You're mortal. You couldn't have known."

Verity's hands clench into fists at her sides, out of sight of Tinle. "Yes, I am mortal."

I slip my fingers into her clenched fists, forcing her hand to relax. "It's perfect, Tinle. I'll take it."

Tinle beams and rattles off a price. "Thank you, Your Grace." He bows as I pass him a purse of gold coin.

With Verity's hand in mine, we duck back out into the street, the silver box safely tucked in my pocket. I help her back into the carriage, noticing the way she visibly relaxes when she's finally out of sight of the Fae in the streets. Night is falling; the roads will soon be filled with Fae celebrations that last long into the night. I smirk, picturing the wild parties that stretch into the early dawn. Verity isn't quite ready for that yet. I eye her as she peers out the window. Maybe someday, but it will have to be a slow introduction.

As the carriage moves on, I settle next to Verity. I put the box in my lap and turn to her. "Turn around," I murmur.

She does as I say, peeking over her shoulder. I brush her hair away gently, my fingers grazing over her lovely porcelain skin. She shudders as I trail my touch over the sharp bones in her neck. If things were different between us, I might press my lips to the back of her neck in a soft kiss. But I won't press her; not when things are so delicate between us.

I drape the necklace over her head until it's settled against her chest. I clasp it, securing it around her neck. Reluctantly, I drop my hands away from her neck and back into my lap. She settles back against the seat and stares down at the necklace on her breast. She runs her hands over the amber stones.

"The color is the same as your eyes," she says softly.

"Is it?" I feign ignorance. "I hardly noticed."

She looks at me suspiciously but then her lips quirk into a smile. "I had no idea this world was so vast and diverse."

"Well, you've only seen a very small corner of it. My kingdom is small in comparison to others as well," I explain. "There's so much to see."

Verity fingers one of the gems. "I'd like to see this river someday."

"Perhaps I can take you," I say, hope swelling in my chest. This is what we need. We need more than my curse to build a relationship on. A thirst for adventure will do. I imagine Verity by my side as we take on the world and grin to myself. She's the only one I would want beside me.

"If you have time," she murmurs. "Being King has kept you busy."

I press my lips together in a thin line. "I'm sorry, Verity."

She falls silent and closes her eyes, as if she's tired. I wait for her to speak, but her lips never part. I leave her and drop my head back against the seat. I will do anything in my power to bring back a smile to Verity's face. I will chase her demons over the ends of the earth to bring her joy again. Something is eating at her, and I need to find out what.

CHAPTER 3

The wind howls through the mountains like a banshee hailing death's arrival. I smile as a pleasant chill trails down my spine. My red cloak snaps in the breeze, the hood flying off to expose my pale blonde hair. In the distance, I can see the night beasts crawling out from the crags in the mountains as the sun sets.

The appearance of the night beasts from their dark and shadowy hiding places always heralds the sunset. They waste no time, even adventuring into dim sunlight to sate their bloodlust. I grin slyly to myself as I watch a pack of them dart after a stray deer. When I was young and free of responsibility, I would follow the hunts on my deadwood broom, just for the joy of seeing the night beasts tear apart their prey's necks.

But there is no more time to waste staring into the barren mountains. Not when Maaz has need of me. I whirl around and stalk back into the Bloodbane keep. A massive fortress built directly into the mountainside; the keep is a monolithic structure of dark grey stone. The walls are huge slabs of stone with few windows. The halls are lit with torches and flaming chandeliers hanging from the tall ceilings. Dark and foreboding, it has been my home for hundreds of years.

I sweep through the halls, past the novice Bloodbane witches that mop the floors and serve us. They bow their heads nervously as I pass but I ignore them. Maaz may have the time and appetite to torture our younger sisters, but I find such obvious entertainment lacking in substance. I prefer unexpected and unpredictable cruelty.

Maaz is in the Holy Rite. I've kept her waiting for an hour. She didn't bother to summon me herself, so I won't bother to do as she commands until it pleases me. The Bloodbane nature is one of obstinance and conflict. It's in our blood.

The Holy Rite is in the top of the keep in the center tower. I sweep up the stairs, glancing through the slivers of windows out into the mountain night. Soon, the night creatures will crawl from the crevices and gullies up the keep walls and we will delight in flaying them. But before then, I must speak with Maaz.

I push open the heavy iron doors and step reverently into the Holy Rite. The room is circular, with giant pillars surrounding the Blood Well in the center. Large doors on either side of the room lead out into the balcony that surrounds the room. The doors are shut now, blocking the heavy winds and rain and the night creatures from creeping into our holiest of places. Torches line the room, filling it with a red glow.

Maaz is in the center, kneeling before the Blood Well. My footsteps are silent as I pad towards her. Her pale blonde hair is braided in a complicated strand, her cloak discarded on the ground next to her. I can feel my blade strapped to my thigh and I imagine how easy it would be to slice into her flesh while she looks away.

Her head snaps towards me when I'm within arm's reach. Her cold blue eyes study me imperiously. "Nice of you to join me, Cleo," she says.

"I am yours to command, sister," I sneer.

She looks away and tilts her chin to the Blood Well. Above it, Sadal Melik's symbol hangs from a heavy chain. No one knows Sadal's true form. When he appears before us, he takes whatever form he wishes. The Bloodbane have depicted him as a seven-horned crocodile for thousands and thousands of years. "Kneel before the Master," she whispers.

I grimace, slipping my gaze towards the empty Blood Well. Maaz is the most devout of our sisterhood. I've never understood her devotion to Sadal. "He isn't one for piousness," I quip. "Tell me why you've brought me here."

"I have failed," Maaz says under her breath. She runs a hand over the rough stone at the lip of the Blood Well.

I narrow my eyes, staring down at her. I told Maaz many years ago when she first cursed Altair that he was not hers to toy with. But she insisted on giving him a thousand years to break his curse. And now he's gone and done it at the last minute. My lip curls as I stare at Maaz's distraught back. She's a fool. I stay silent, waiting for Maaz to speak. I have nothing to say that could bring her any comfort.

"I have failed my sisters and I have failed my Master," she mumbles. I watch as she withdraws a knife from her thin shift. She holds it over her narrow wrist. "I am not fit to be the Master's bride."

She plunges the knife to her skin while I grin. I let her draw a drop of blood before snatching the dagger from her hand. She gasps and glowers up at me. "Don't be such a fool," I snap. "If Sadal wanted you dead you wouldn't be kneeling before the Blood Well."

Bloodbane that disappoint or betray our Master are often found in a pool of their own blood in the bottom of the shallow Blood Well with no clues as to how they came to be there. Sadal wouldn't be pleased if Maaz took her own life. He would consider it a stolen life – that he was robbed of punishing her himself. I stare back up at the crocodile head hanging above us. It grins down at me with sharp iron teeth.

"Give me my dagger so I can follow His will," Maaz snarls.

I toss the dagger between my hands. Maaz has always had a flair for the dramatic, it's part of what made her such a great ruler for the Bloodbane. Most Bloodbane queens barely survive three hundred years before they're murdered by another. But not Maaz. She's far too clever for that. I prefer to keep my head, so I play my part in the background of the tapestry of life. Maaz could never bear to be out of the spotlight. I study the streak of blood on the blade.

"You haven't a fool's idea of what his will is, Maaz," I say coolly. "You haven't spoken to him for a thousand years, not since he told you his plans for the Fae."

She stiffens. "I know what Sadal requires of those who fail him."

"So you plan to give up then?" I quip, tossing her the blade. "Such a shame that his First Bride is too weak to try again."

Maaz narrows her eyes at me. "Why do you care if I live or die? The rest of our sisters would have plunged the blade into my heart with a smile."

I chuckle. "Trust me, I thought about it. It makes me sick to see you so weak. You've grown spoiled. One thing doesn't go your way and you're ready to die. It's pathetic."

"Then what would you suggest, Cleo? Since you're so clever," Maaz snarls.

"What's the old adage? A failure is only permanent if you stop trying?" I inspect my nails. "Something like that anyway."

"Your suggestion is to try again?" Maaz rolls her eyes. "How brilliant."

I smile to myself. I've at least stopped Maaz from sacrificing herself for her failure. It doesn't matter what comes next as long as she lives on. "We have eternity to carry on with Sadal's will."

"We work on the Dark God's timeline," Maaz snaps. "There is no time to waste."

My eyes narrow at her words. The Bloodbane are not a notoriously hurried people. We do what we want, when we want expect at the will of Sadal. As a soulless immortal, I've never felt pressed for time. And yet, Maaz is wild-eyed and sincere. She's hiding something.

"I can't support you if I don't know what's going on," I whisper.

Maaz purses her lips. "When Sadal wants to reveal his secrets, he will."

I curl my lip at her. "You and our Dark God can keep your secrets, then."

Maaz ignores me and moves to the door to call for one of the novices. I lean against one of the pillars as the novice in her bright red cloak shuffles inside. The pillars are engraved with images of our sacrifices in the Holy Rite and our rituals. Rituals of which this young girl will soon be a part. She bows deeply to Maaz and then to me, the picture of obeisance. But I can see her keen eyes glittering beneath her hood. Women and girls don't join the Bloodbane because they're meek and humble servants. They join the Bloodbane to satisfy their cravings for power, lust, and death.

"Come, child," Maaz croons, taking the girl by the hand.

I watch as she leads the young woman into the depths of the Blood Well, directly beneath the symbol of Sadal. Maaz draws the novice's hood back, revealing her shining black hair. Maaz cups her cheeks. "What a beauty you are," she murmurs. "Sadal will be pleased."

The girl shivers as Maaz loosens the tie of her cloak and lets it fall to the ground. Novices wear simple cotton dresses, not thick enough to protect her against the chill in the air. Maaz's fingers trail down the girl's arms, and she leans closer to Maaz. With a kind smile, Maaz brushes the novice's hair away from her face and presses a kiss to her cheek.

I see the silver glint of the dagger in her hands. Maaz slices through the air while the girl is distracted, cutting through the thin dress. It falls on top of the cloak, leaving the woman shivering and naked in the red glow of the Blood Well. My own blood is thrumming, singing as power fills the room. The air vibrates with it. The girl sways, her eyes rolling back into her head. She cries out, a lusty shout, as Maaz drags the blade across her throat.

Blood spills from the gouge in her throat, it pours from her lips. With wide eyes, she drops to her knees. Maaz steps out of the Blood Well and joins me beside the lip. The novice's eyes are locked on us as her body shudders once. Her life force pours freely into the Well, filling it as Maaz and I hum our throaty song.

I can feel the air change in the Holy Rite. It's growing warm now; hot even. The light flares brilliantly before growing dim as shadows creep from the edges of the room. I feel a thrill course through my body, I can't help my desire to serve the Dark God and please him. I try to overcome the urges growing in my body, reminding myself that Sadal is unpleasant enough. I need to keep my wits about me when he's with us.

Maaz and I collapse to our knees at the same time, pain shoots through my bones. "My lovely brides," Sadal's sultry voice echoes towards us from the shadows.

Maaz's breath hitches in her throat with a happy sob. She remains on her knees, bowing to him as he approaches. Sadal's shining black boots are splattered in blood as he strides through the Blood Well. He steps on the novice's body carelessly. I peer up at him, taking in the pale ivory skin, the thick black hair and handsome features.

"Get up, darling Maaz," he murmurs, helping her to her feet.

"Master," Maaz whispers. She lifts her head to meet his gaze.

I feel the impact of his palm against her cheek as if Sadal hit me himself. The sound echoes through the Holy Rite. I stand stiffly beside Maaz as she cups her cheek in shock. Sadal paces in front of us. "Did you think you could summon me here and all would be forgotten?" He asks. "Did you think I hadn't noticed your constant failures?"

"Dark One," Maaz says, trying not to stammer. "I know I have failed you. I will offer myself to you now for forgiveness. Kill me."

I curl my lip at her pathetic begging. Sadal turns slowly towards her, calculated and cunning. His black eyes rove over Maaz, a disgusted sneer on his lips. I watch carefully, silently, knowing my hood hides my face from his view. It's a small comfort, the anonymity the hood provides in front of the Dark God. He and I are more alike than I prefer, we both find groveling distasteful.

"Enough," he snaps. "Enough of your groveling. We have work to do."

CHAPTER 4

The sun has set over the sea, and the castle is lit with lamps and torches. The light glitters over the patio where Verity and I are eating dinner. From the patio, Verity can gaze over the wall towards the city and harbor, sparkling in the night. The silence is heavy between us, and I know Verity's mind is preoccupied with questions about her past and future. She's looking for answers that I can't give her, and it kills me.

Bird song floats through the night air, accompanied by the chirping of crickets. The only other sound is the clatter of silverware against porcelain. I watch as Verity slips a piece of steak between her lips. Her eyes are locked onto the glowing horizon and the sails that mar it.

"Where are the ships from?" She asks, breaking the silence between us.

"Berenices, Mensa, and Canes," I say. "Those are merchant ships."

"What did they bring?" Verity turns back to her meal.

I cluck my tongue, trying to remember the contents of the

meeting I was in only yesterday. "Spices from Berenices, wine from Mensa, and wheat from Canes," I say thoughtfully. "They're the first merchants to return to Desmarais since the curse was lifted."

Verity takes a sip of her wine and runs a hand over the necklace at her throat. "I'm glad."

I swallow hard, nodding in agreement. Verity's eyes are glazed over, as if she hardly listened to my explanation. I inhale sharply. I can't really blame her, but I know that two weeks ago, Verity would have smiled broadly at the news that Alnembra was returning to the world. This strange creature across from me is only an echo of Verity. "Do you think you're ready?" I ask, eyeing her.

"For what?" She raises her brows.

I purse my lips, suddenly nervous. "To fulfill the covenant you made with me. To marry me."

She blanches, biting her bottom lip. I stare, thinking of the few times we shared passion between us. Passion that I've been craving. Verity doesn't answer, instead downing her full goblet of wine. Irritation sparks in my chest as she dodges the question so obviously. I had such high hopes, hopes that I've been clinging to for weeks now.

"Why did you return?" I ask suddenly, my words cutting through the air between us.

She looks up, startled, and then drops my gaze. "I wanted to help."

"And now have you changed your mind?" I press, eyes flashing.

"No," she mumbles. "Why do you ask?"

"When you came here against your will, you were wild and fiery and stubborn. All I see before me now is a mute doll," I snap. "I thought things between us were different, that we could at least be friends, if not more. But since the curse has broken, it seems that something inside you broke as well."

She narrows her blue eyes and I feel a sense of satisfaction that I at least inspired her to feel something beyond apathy. "You have no idea how I feel, and you haven't even bothered to ask," she says, a vicious hiss to her words.

I close my eyes, thinking of the moments I spent at Verity's side, waiting for her to confide in me. She's right. I did little to reassure her. I've been so preoccupied with treating her like a fragile doll, that I didn't let her speak. When I open my eyes again, the anger has ebbed.

"Tell me how you feel," I say gently. "I can't stand to see you so sorrowful."

"You wouldn't understand," she mutters, picking at her food.

"Verity, I can at least try," I say forcefully as I shove my food aside.

Verity purses her lips at the sudden movement. "When you invited me for dinner, I wasn't expecting a fight."

"Neither was I," I laugh mirthlessly. I quiet, fingers tracing the bulge in the pocket of my tunic. "I invited you here for a romantic evening. I invited you here to give you this."

I pull a small black box from my pocket and pass it across the table towards her. She takes it tentatively, her fingers closing around it as if it was poisonous. I watch her brows furrow as she opens the box. Inside, she finds a ring with a pearl setting. Verity lifts it and studies it in the candlelight. Her eyes widen slightly, as if she expected it but never quite accepted the possibility. I never expected a joyous cry from her, but I didn't expect her to grimace either.

Verity's lips twist into a reluctant frown as she fingers the engagement ring. I lean forward, hands clasped. "Verity, your covenant to me has led us to this moment. Will you marry me?"

"Marry you?" She echoes.

I purse my lips, frustration coiling in my chest. This was not how I envisioned this moment, and my planned speech is useless now. "Yes. Will you marry me?" I repeat stubbornly.

"I knew when I covenanted with you that I had promised something like this," she murmurs. "I accept the consequences."

"Consequences," I chuckle, eyes flashing. "There was a time I imagined things between us much differently."

"Things have changed," Verity says coolly. "I have changed. No matter how I much I grew to like you, I never wanted to be engaged so quickly after my last relationship ended. And I- I'm different now. Inside."

"You aren't a Bloodbane," I snap, slamming a fist on the table. "Just because that oath runs in your veins doesn't mean you need to become like them. If you're with me, you'll never be like them. You'll be safe."

She purses her lips as if holding back. "Then who will I be? The Curse-Breaker? The almost witch?"

"You'll be mine," I whisper, softening. "You'll be Verity."

Verity stands, smoothing out the wrinkles in her silk gown. "I don't know who that is anymore, Altair."

She sweeps away before I can speak. Her back is stiff and her shoulders straight. She looks like a woman fighting against some internal force or compulsion. She looks like she's breaking. Half way across the patio, she stumbles, clutching at her gut. I lunge to my feet, ready to run for her, but she pushes through the doors before I get the chance.

I glance across the table to her half-eaten plate. The ring is gone, though I never saw her slip it onto her finger. I clench my fists, anger and shame sweeping through me. I should have knelt. I should have put it on her finger myself. I should have told her everything I planned to say. All the words I carefully wrote about how my heart gradually opened to hers, until it was only her that could fill it will never be voiced. I curse softly under my breath. I'm a fool, and I let my frustration get the best of me on this important night. This night should have been about Verity; about our future together. I rise, my chair clattering to the floor.

I run across the patio, following Verity. The servants and my councilors watch me curiously as I sprint past them, but I ignore them. I take the stairs to Verity's room two at a time, streaking past Navi. I find Verity just outside her room, breathing hard. My heart squeezes painfully in my chest as I see her. She shouldn't be walking so much without her cane. But if I mention her reliance on the thin wood, she wouldn't be pleased. I've already done enough damage tonight.

She glances at me over her shoulder and chews her bottom lip. "What do you want, Altair? I'm tired."

I slip past her and open the door wordlessly. I know that no matter what I say, she'll find something to stand against. She stares stubbornly at me before taking my hand and letting me lead her to one of the armchairs by the fire. She sinks into it with a sigh and I kneel in front of her, my hands on her knees. Desire floods through me as I stare up at her, taking in her full lips and lovely eyes.

"Verity," I murmur hoarsely.

A blush creeps to her cheeks at the throaty lust in my voice. "Altair?"

I force my desire back, reminding myself of the brief argument we just had. And reminding myself that Verity doesn't want me anymore. I'm merely a consequence. I sober quickly. "I came to explain more clearly what your covenant to me means."

"I know what it means," she says, brows furrowing.

"I, Verity Chastain, bind my life to yours. I will give you all of me. I will make my vows to you instead of the Dark God," I say softly, repeating the words she said to me weeks ago as she lay in a pool of her own blood.

"I know what I said." She blushes.

I rub my thumb over her knee gently. "When the Bloodbane witches become what they are, they marry the Dark God. When Maaz cursed me, she told me that only a Bloodbane that could betray the Dark God could save me. You are the only one, Verity, who was able to do that. Once a Bloodbane covenants with Sadal Melik, she is his for eternity. But you, you had a choice. And you chose me."

Verity bites her lip and closes her eyes tightly. "Is marriage the only way?"

"It is the best way," I say softly. "You could sacrifice your life for me through death, or you could bear me children."

She blanches. "Children or death. You are being merciful indeed offering me marriage instead."

"It isn't mercy," I say fiercely. "I care for you."

"I know that I've grown distant," Verity stammers. "But nothing between you and I has changed. At least not truly."

Relief floods through me at her words. "I'm sorry I grew so frustrated at you. That was unacceptable."

"And your proposal was disappointing." She smiles tentatively, the first smile I've seen from her since we returned from Desmarais after she exhausted herself.

My lips quirk into a grin. "Verity, will you do me the great honor of becoming my wife?"

She pulls the engagement ring from her pocket and places it in my outstretched hand. Wordlessly she holds out her thin hand and I slip the ring onto an elegant finger. "I will," she says, her eyes clouded with some inexplicable emotion.

I lift off of my knees enough to kiss her brow. I feel her stiffen beneath the brief touch, but she doesn't draw away from me – a good sign. "It looks lovely on you."

"It's a beautiful ring," she murmurs, lifting it to the light.

"It's a replica of my mother's," I explain, a melancholy smile on my lips.

"A replica?" She echoes.

I purse my lips and then settle myself. "Her body was never recovered, but I had your ring modeled exactly after hers."

Her brows wrinkle sympathetically. "I'm sorry, I forgot."

I shake my head, waving away her apology. I gaze up at her pale blue eyes and soft, brown hair. She's beautiful. I only miss when those eyes were filled fire instead of sorrow. I reach for a decanter of wine and pour us both a drink. Verity accepts and takes a small sip. I smile, remembering the first ball she attended and how she guzzled the wine so nervously.

"We will have a ball, celebrating our engagement," I say, lifting my cup with a grin.

Verity's lips twist. "Altair," she says stubbornly. "You remember the last one. Do you have to have one?"

I drape myself into the armchair next to her and laugh. "I must. Trust me, Verity, it will be fun."

"How long until the ball?" She asks.

"A week's time," I say, enjoying the way she gapes. I've been planning this ball for days already, all the preparations are made. "Just in time for Summer's Eve, and your wound should be healed as well."

Verity slumps back in her chair. "I should start practicing. You're too busy to be my dancing partner. I suppose a guard will have to do."

Anger flares within me as I imagine her wrapped in another man's arms, twirling through the room. "Absolutely not," I snarl. "Navi will be your tutor."

"Navi?" Verity snorts. "I doubt she'll agree to it."

"She'll agree because I'll tell her to," I growl.

Verity raises a brow, and it's as if I get a glimpse of the woman I grew to love weeks ago. But it disappears just as quickly. "I'm tired," she murmurs.

I run my tongue over my lips, disappointment flaring. But I don't want to press her, I don't want to force her to tolerate my presence. I rise slowly to my feet and set my goblet aside. I leave her by the fire, staring into its depths. At the door, I turn back to her and catch her staring forlornly at the ring on her finger.

Sorrow and trepidation coil in my chest and my gut twists at the sight.

Wordlessly, I close the door and pause in the dim light of the hall. I lean my head against her door, brows furrowed. For a moment, I pictured her happy. But I was wrong.

CHAPTER 5

VERITY

The early morning sun sparkles on the morning dew that glistens on the grass and leaves throughout the garden. I wander across the lawn to the small grove of trees where I had my first true conversation with Acubens – Altair – weeks ago. My boots are almost soaked through already with dew as I trod across the lawn.

My fingers trail over the foliage of the trees as I pass. I catch a glimpse of the ring on my finger. The pearl is a perfect setting, ringed by small clear crystals on a thin silver band. My heart clenches as I stare at the engagement ring. It's a significant ring, not simply because it signifies my impending marriage to Altair, but because it's modeled after the ring his mother wore. He had this made especially for me.

I bite my lip, my stomach twisting with nerves. Altair and I have become different people now. It's almost strange how much we've changed in only a few weeks. But we have changed. He's grown more lively, a little kinder. And I've become lost. He knows. He knows and he'll try to fix me. But I don't know if I can be fixed. And I doubt the wedding will bring me the kind of answers and comfort I need. My questions are of the sort that only another Bloodbane could answer.

Only a little while ago, I was at my own wedding. And now I'll have another – who knows how soon. I'm grateful that Altair dragged me away from my wedding that morning. It made me realize how much I truly didn't want to be with Henry and how I wasn't prepared to be married. I tell myself it will be different with Altair, but truthfully, I don't know. It's the not knowing that scares me.

A loud slamming sound drags me from my thoughts. I glance up, staring through the trees towards the palace doors. Servants are carrying a set of wooden beams through, no doubt some kind of decoration for the ball tonight. The week I've had to prepare for the ball hasn't left me anymore confident than I was last time. Navi was impatient in her tutelage and seemed eager to be done with the lessons. But so was I.

Dancing and being a pleasant princess to the Fae who will be in attendance just doesn't seem important right now. I'm more concerned with my own identity. Ever since I committed myself to Altair, I've felt like my blood is filled with lead.

I turn away from the preparations and move deeper into the grove of trees. The sound of birds has disappeared, and the wind is quiet. Slowly, I catch the sound of snapping scissors. Curious, I follow it towards the shadows by the wall that borders the palace. I narrow my eyes, trying to pierce the gloom. Despite Altair's victory over the Bloodbane, he's warned me to be careful even on palace grounds. Apprehension grips me as I follow the light snipping sound.

I push aside a large tree branch, just I catch a flash of silver streaking towards me. I yelp and lurch backwards as the enormous shears slice through the branch where my hand was. A Fae man pokes his head through the leaves, his brows wrinkled with concern. My heart leaps as I recognize him from earlier in the week. It's the gardener I saw before Altair and I went into Desmarais.

His dark hair is combed back away from his face, leaves trapped in the fine locks. His dark eyes rove over me as he drops the scissors. "Curse-Breaker," he stammers, bowing sharply. "I'm so sorry. I didn't hear you approach. Are you alright?"

"I'm fine," I say breathlessly, unable to drag my eyes away from his black gaze.

"Please forgive me, Curse-Breaker. I didn't think anyone would come to this part of the garden while I pruned it and I grew careless," he says. His voice is deep and laced with a smooth accent.

"Please don't call me Curse-Breaker," I say, heart pounding wildly. "My name is Verity."

"Verity," he murmurs, smiling. His dark eyes flash and my heart skips a beat. "Call me Dain."

He disappears back into the foliage, glancing at me over his shoulder with a magnetic gaze. I follow, curiosity gripping me. Behind the wall of leaves that he was clipping, is a small clearing. Iridescent, green light filters through the leaves above. He pauses in the center, in shadow, his eyes glimmering. There's a wheelbarrow beside him filled with tools. Dain gently places his gardening shears into the wheelbarrow and then takes a seat. I stare, surprised, as he lounges back against a tree. His smiles pleasantly and gestures for me to join him.

Brows furrowed, I sit cross-legged across from him. He stares at me, and I shift awkwardly, wondering what he sees. "So, you don't like being called Curse-Breaker," he muses.

"No." I shake my head. "I didn't really do much. It just feels undeserved."

He purses his lips thoughtfully. "That's your perspective. Imagine that the Fae in Alnembra have been trapped for a thousand years, waiting for to die from a curse that can't be broken.

Even if you feel as if the admiration is undeserved, they'll forever be in your debt."

"I suppose," I murmur. "I can't imagine what it's like to live for a thousand years."

He plucks at the nearby grass and then lets the blades drift from his pale fingers. "Life can be so short," he says, staring at the blades.

"Well when you tear it apart like that, you shouldn't be surprised," I say, surprised by my own brazenness.

Dain laughs, tossing his head back. "You're right."

"Will you be alright, taking a break like this?" I ask, glancing around.

"These gardens will be here for centuries more; the branches will continue to grow and I'll still be here to trim them. A few moments won't hurt," he says.

His words remind me of what Altair told me before taking me into the city. Life goes on. And when you're Fae, time is almost meaningless. "It must be nice," I murmur. "Living life without a deadline over your head."

"I forgot that you're mortal," he says, his eyes flickering with curiosity.

"And I forget that the Fae live for thousands of years." I smile. I wonder if marrying Altair is truly the right thing. I will grow old, while he'll remain young and limber.

"There are some that live even longer. There are some that live forever," Dain says slyly.

My brows furrow. "Who?"

"The old gods." Dain gestures at our surroundings, as if they're right next to us.

"I don't know anything about the old gods of this world," I say. My eyes narrow with curiosity. "We have different gods in mine."

Dain shrugs. "There are many who don't follow the old gods anymore, like Altair."

"What do you know of Altair?" I ask, curiosity gripping me. I don't miss the casual way he neglects Altair's title.

He leans forward. "Altair knows the old gods exist, he simple refuses to honor them."

I press my lips together thoughtfully. "Altair and I have never discussed it."

"And yet you're engaged to be wed," Dain says, cocking a brow.

"Because of the curse. I won't bore you with the details. But I had to agree to marry him to break the curse," I explain, trying to keep it simple as a blush creeps over my cheeks.

"How?" Dain asks eagerly. "I've been so curious."

I blanch and turn my eyes away. I don't like it when the Fae look at me like that; like I'm something special. "I'm a Bloodbane, or at least, I could be. But I haven't made my covenants with Sadal Melik yet, and instead I will make them with Altair."

"Altair isn't a god." Dain looks confused.

"No," I say hesitantly. "But I suppose it doesn't matter. The curse broke anyway."

"Is that what you prefer?" Dain asks. "To be covenanted with Altair instead of Sadal Melik?"

My eyes narrow. I think of the witches that kidnapped me weeks ago. "Of course. I know enough about Sadal Melik to know he's evil. And Maaz isn't any better." I shudder, remembering the cold slice of her blade in my gut. "I don't want to be like them."

Dain nods apologetically. "Of course, forgive me. It's not often that a Fae meets a Bloodbane."

He was merely curious. I can understand that. I loose a breath. "It's alright. How long have you been a gardener here? I haven't seen you before."

"I worked here before the curse took hold. But then I left to be with my family for that time. The king didn't want many servants left behind," Dain explains.

I hear rustling in the trees behind me. I twist, staring into the foliage to see if any of Altair's soldiers are approaching. But the small grove is empty. "I should go," I say softly.

"Why?" Dain's brows crumple.

"Altair gets jealous easily," I say, rolling my eyes. "I saw him nearly tear apart a guard for making me laugh."

"Is there a reason for him to be jealous? I don't recall making you laugh yet," Dain says.

I smile. "Who knows, your philosophical musings might amuse me one day."

"A man can hope," he says, winking.

I blink, wondering if I simply imagined the subtle movement. "It was nice meeting you, Dain."

He rises, bowing shallowly. "Verity," he says, stopping me from leaving. "I wouldn't matter to me how Altair punished me for talking to you, I would do it again."

I bite my lip, cheeks flushing. "Strong words from a man who hasn't faced the consequences yet."

"Find me again," he calls as I step through the foliage.

I don't answer, my heart beating wildly as I hurry away from the small clearing. Soon, the birds start chirping again. I linger at the edge of the grove of trees, just beside the lawn leading to the palace. The preparations are still underway, the servants carrying in massive sheets of silk and various decorations to outfit the ballroom with.

The sun is high in the sky now and I wonder how much time passed while I spoke with Dain. My heart clenches in my chest as I picture the handsome gardener in my mind. He's flirtatious and charming, but he's honest. I can see bits of Altair in him, but he's much kinder. I bite my lip as my thoughts drift around Dain.

I feel a surge of heat in my core and I blush. It's been weeks since I felt desire for anyone. I've spent too much time pitying myself over my injury and worrying about who I truly am. But somehow, just the thought of Dain and his mysterious smile can draw those sensations up in me again. Something not even Altair and his soft kisses have been able to do yet.

I hurry into the palace, trying to put some distance between Dain and me. But my eyes burn with excitement and I feel more alive than I have since the night Maaz arrived. My blood is singing, the heaviness gone. My thoughts aren't plagued with questions about my future while they flit around Dain. Somehow, he's freed me from the fear that I've carried on my shoulders since the night I broke the curse. I pause at one of the windows looking over the front lawn. I see Dain in the shadows by the trees, his eyes latched onto me. My breath hitches in my throat as our eyes lock. He smiles, and I can't help but smile back.

CHAPTER 6

ALTAIR

Music floats from the ballroom doors as a string quartet plays ambient music for the arriving guests. The halls of the castle are lit brilliantly with lamplight, decorated in bundles of wild flowers. I pace along the soft carpet, out of sight of my guests as I wait for Verity. I didn't have much time to spend with her this week; there are rumors that the Bloodbane are stirring again.

I curse under my breath. I had hoped it would take them more than a few short weeks to mobilize again. I drag a hand over my cleanly shaved chin with a sigh. The ball to mark Summer's Eve is a tradition among the Fae, where summer is our most-loved season. But with the Bloodbane, my wedding, and Verity's strange behavior, I wonder if I should have skipped it this year.

I hear a soft cough echo from the stairs. I glance up sharply. I was so preoccupied with my thoughts; I didn't hear Verity approaching. She stands at the top of the stairs. Once she would have stared imperiously down at me, but now her shoulders curl inwards. I bite my lip, taking in her beauty as she descends the stairs.

Dressed in a blush pink gown of tulle, she looks like a cloud at dawn. Her brown hair is braided away from her face but spilling over her back and bare shoulders. I stare at the porcelain skin of her neck, imagining dragging my tongue over it. A low growl rumbles from my chest and Verity blushes. Biting my lip with a grin, I take her hand and circle her predatorially.

"You look lovely," I murmur.

"Thank you," she says softly. Her shoulders straighten slightly, as if she's gaining more confidence.

I take in the way she doesn't double over her belly anymore. Her wound will have fully healed by now, leaving only a pale scar. Verity is a vision in the gown, and I know all I'll be able to think about tonight is her. I already have half a mind to skip the ball and drag her up to my room. "It's a beautiful gown," I purr, slipping a hand around her waist. "It will be a shame to see it torn to shreds after the ball."

Her lips part slightly in surprise and her cheeks flush. But her eyes light with fire, sending desire pulsing through me. Wordlessly, I take her arm and lead her to the ballroom doors. She hesitates, but then straightens her shoulders and takes a deep breath. From the corner of my eye, I see her thumb picking at the ring on her left hand.

The doors swing wide and we step through into the bright light of the ballroom. The crystal chandeliers that hang from the ceiling are lit brilliantly. Flowers adorn nearly every free surface. It feels as if we've stepped into the gardens instead of the ballroom. A massive arch has been constructed by my servants near the other end of the hall. It's draped in silk and wild flowers.

Verity inhales sharply as we descend the short steps into the crowd. Verity leans close to me, her bare shoulder brushing against my navy-blue jacket. "They didn't announce you," she whispers.

"It's Summer's Eve," I murmur. "Their focus is elsewhere."

"But do they know we're engaged?" Her brows furrow with confusion.

"They do." I slip an arm around her waist and sweep her onto the dance floor. "And we will revel in it later. But for now, dance with me."

The Fae along the sidelines watch as Verity and I take the first steps in a waltz. Her eyes flit over the Fae guests, worry clear in her blue irises. I sweep her into a spin before she can think about the Fae filling the ballroom. She gasps softly and I grin. Later tonight, when we're alone, perhaps I can make her gasp like that again.

Verity notices the wild gleam in my eyes and blushes. She nearly stumbles over the steps, but I carry her through it smoothly. With Verity in my arms, it's as if everything else in the world melts away. We might as well be alone in the ballroom, the only two people in the entire world. She may be drifting away from me, but I will do everything in my power to draw her back.

The song ends, and I step into a waltz pose with Verity. The crowd erupts into applause, but it's short-lived and the music starts up again. The Fae don't hesitate before crowding onto the dance floor. Bright smiles split their faces and my servants slip through the crowds with flutes of spirits for my guests. Summer's Eve can be riotous even among the noble Fae, I hope Verity will enjoy it.

With her hand in mine, we drift through the crowd to the fringes of the room so she can take a breath. Verity's fingers twist the ring on her finger. "This is different from last time," she notes, staring apprehensively at the Fae.

I watch as they drink and laugh, practically shouting. A few of the women have already stripped out of their fine gowns and are swaying, naked, in the crowd. "The Fae used to be one with nature, we lived in meadows and streams, naked as the day we were born. But we've drifted away from such ways of life. We still honor our origins with Summer's Eve and Winter's Night," I explain, eyes raking over one of the swaying Fae.

"So, all those legends about the wildness of the Fae are true," Verity says, cocking a brow.

"Were true," I correct her. "Now, we only return to our roots when we've had plenty to drink."

She snatches a goblet of wine from a passing servant and takes a long drink. "I guess I need to get very drunk then."

I chuckle, imagining Verity's awkward human frame dancing the old and aggressive ways of the Fae. "You aren't joining them," I say, a smile playing at my lips.

"Why not? You have centuries more to get naked and party like this. I have only a few more years before I'll be too wrinkly to dance nude in a crowd," she says, arching a brow.

"You aren't joining them because the pleasure of seeing you stripped of this finery is mine and mine alone," I purr, bending over her ear. "Why should strangers enjoy what I haven't?"

She shivers, biting her lip, and then suddenly rounds on me. "I'm not your property," she says angrily.

"Of course not." I shrug. "You musn't forget the instincts of the Fae. You remember how territorial I can be."

"Like an animal." She narrows her eyes, as if to insult me.

I grin. "Perhaps."

Verity steps closer to the crowd, her fingers tugging at her skirts. "Maybe I'll join them now."

"Verity," I say warningly.

She eyes me as her hands finger the buttons on the back of her gown. "It looks like fun."

I glance towards the crowd. Already, the music has changed, taking on a more wild tune. The Fae are drinking with abandon, laughing ferally. Verity can't go down there. She would be trampled in their drunken stupor. I cut her off before she can turn and see how the dancing has devolved. I press against her, forcing her back.

"You will not join them," I snarl. "You will stay here with me."

"Stop telling me what to do," she snaps.

"It's for your own good," I say quietly, letting her peek around me to see the Fae.

Her eyes widen as she takes in their nakedness and the wild dancing. "Altair, why the hell have you brought me here if you're just going to keep me trapped on the sidelines?"

"I forgot what Summer's Eve can be like." I meet her stubborn gaze. "I'll stay close to you and they'll gather near the arch, that's what it's for."

Verity brightens. "Does this mean I can leave?"

I purse my lips. "No."

She rolls her eyes and takes another sip of her wine. "You're such a hard ass sometimes."

I feel a thread of satisfaction as Verity returns to her normal self. The subdued, anxious Verity has all but disappeared. I missed her sass and her stubborn nature; this is a welcome change. I can't resist taking her in my arms, the atmosphere of Summer's Eve is already clouding my mind. The Fae don't need spirits to fall into the giddy haze of summer's call, but alcohol certainly helps.

I nuzzle her neck, letting the fog of the wild overtake me. Verity stiffens in my arms, and then suddenly eases into me. A thrill courses through me. I nip at her neck and she gasps softly. I don't care that Verity and I can be seen by the entirety of Fae nobility and my foreign guests. The last thing on my mind is prudence. The music escalates and I hear the Fae shrieking wildly in the background.

I bury my hands in her tulle skirts to clutch her ass. Her arms wrap around me tightly as I drive her back against the pillar. The wildness in me wants her right now, to take her while the music is at its peak and the moonlight shines through the windows. I growl low, trying to restrain myself even as I fight to give into the urge. I don't know if it's the wine she drank, or if the atmosphere of Summer's Eve has affected her too, but Verity is supple in my hands.

She shivers as I drag my tongue across her jugular. It's been too long since I kissed this woman. Too long since I felt her heat in my arms. She writhes against me, panting, and I grin ferally. Suddenly, I feel a sharp tug at my collar, and I'm ripped away from Verity's body. I stumble, catching myself before I fall into the crowd.

Navi glowers at me, one hand on her sword while I glare at her. "Altair," she says firmly. "Get a grip."

I snarl. "Back away, Navi. She's mine."

"I don't want your mortal," Navi hisses.

I clench my hands into fists at my side, wishing I had a weapon with me. Suddenly, Navi strikes me. My cheek stings painfully with the force of her slap. She narrows her eyes at me and tucks her hand behind her back as if to hide it. But the pain and the shock have had the intended effect. I blink and stare at Navi in surprise. It's been centuries since Navi last struck me.

I glance towards Verity. Her skirts are wrinkled, her hair mussed, and her cheeks are flushed pink. I feel a wave of shame seeing what I've done to her in front of the Fae. Verity isn't one of us. She isn't as animalistic as we are. I drop my chin and take a deep breath.

"I'm sorry, Verity," I say.

"It's okay," she stammers.

"It's not," I snap. "I have to go."

"Go?" Verity follows me up the steps towards the doors. She clutches at my jacket. "You told me you wouldn't leave me. Where are you going?"

I tear my arm out of her hands, feeling the well of desire growing in me again. "I can't be here with you, Verity. I can hardly think straight. You've sworn yourself to me and I-I don't know if I can stop myself."

"Stop yourself from doing what?" She asks, reaching for me again.

I dart out of reach of her elegant fingers. "I'll come back when I've calmed down."

She inhales sharply, eyes filled with worry. "Please don't leave me here."

"Navi," I say, ignoring Verity's words. "Find Thal and keep Verity close to you."

"Thal?" Verity's brow wrinkles.

"Thal can keep his head better than I," I say softly. "I'll be back."

I spin away and bound out of the ballroom, leaving Verity behind. My heart clenches in my chest as I fight against the urge to return to her. But I know that if I do, I'll just fall back into the haze of desire. I stalk away from the ballroom and lean against the wall.

In the past, I used to dive into the revelry of Summer's Eve. I would celebrate our past with the others, dancing under the arch of flowers. I would even find a Fae woman, sometimes more than one. But it's been hundreds of years since I celebrated Summer's Eve, and I lost my head to the haze. It was stupid of me to bring Verity to the celebration, stupid of me to think it would be just like any ball. The Fae haven't celebrated Summer's Eve like this in years, they will throw themselves into the cloud of Summer's Eve without a second thought.

Navi is stronger than most, more stubborn. She can resist the temptation as well as the older Fae. Despite Thal's playboy nature, he's never participated in Summer's Eve. I trust them more than myself to take care of Verity. She has to stay for the length of the party. When the moon sets, I'll announce our engagement.

"Your Grace," a voice says behind me.

I twist, taking in the messenger standing in the hall. He leans imperceptibly towards the music floating towards us from the closed ballroom doors. "What is it?" I ask, my voice hoarse.

"I have news for you from your general on the border,

General Kane," the messenger says. "While patrolling, he found one of the guard towers in ruin."

"Ruin?" I sober up immediately. The towers along the border have always been repaired throughout the years, even during the curse. We've never let one of our precious protections against the Bloodbane fall into disrepair.

The messenger bows. "He said it was completely destroyed and there were no signs of the soldiers stationed there," he says seriously.

I press my lips into a thin line. "You may go."

"Yes, Your Grace." The messenger runs off down the hall.

I pace the hall, picturing the crumbling guard tower. We only have one enemy that would dare to do something like this; the Bloodbane. I curl my lip as I think of Maaz. She won't crawl into a hole and give up after being defeated. Whatever her plan, I know she won't rest until she's destroyed every Fae in Alnembra, and perhaps the world.

Fury lances through me as I picture her giving the order to destroy the tower. A message for me, telling me that nothing will stop her from taking what she wants. Her curse failed, the lazy way of leading my kingdom to ruin failed her. Now she'll try to take over my kingdom in a more traditional way – a more violent way.

If she wants a war, I'll give her one.

CHAPTER 7

CLEO

The chill wind of the summer night pricks at my fingertips as I clutch the hilt of my deadwood broom. I squeeze the wood tighter, ignoring the pain of the frigid air. Below me, Altair's palace is sprawled out and glowing with lights. Carriages trundle up the long drive and music floats up into the sky to reach my ears.

The hood of my blood red cloak is drawn up to protect me from the chill. The light fabric rustles in the wind. The young Bloodbane beside me sighs dramatically, as if our mission here isn't interesting enough. I scowl. Even Maaz doesn't appear particularly interested in Altair's movements. Since we summoned Sadal, she has had eyes for him alone. I've taken it upon myself to study our enemy for weaknesses. Maaz has grown complacent, too proud to see how dangerous a war with Altair could be.

I watch as a group of Fae women prance up the steps and into the palace, their thin gowns shimmering in the starlight. I sigh through my nose at the sight of them. There was once a time when Maaz and I celebrated Summer's Eve with the wildest of the Fae. Their parties were never truly enough to sate us. We preferred the old ways – the violent and bloody sacrifices, the lusty rutting. Now, we don't celebrate Summer's Eve at all.

I lean forward, careful not to drive my deadwood broom any closed to the ground. The celebration is in full swing. I wonder briefly if the Curse-Breaker is enjoying it, or if she's frightened. I grin viciously, picturing the tiny mortal quivering in the corner. Mortals aren't fit to reside with the Fae, and they certainly aren't fit to join the ranks of the Bloodbane. And yet, Sadal wants her. He wants every Bloodbane.

He won't be pleased when he hears that they've announced they're engagement. The young witch beside me flies in slow circles to ease her boredom. I snap my teeth at her and narrow my eyes. She freezes, paling at my furious gaze. The more she moves, the more likely it is that we'll be spotted in these clouds.

"Why isn't Maaz here?" The young witch asks after a moment of nervous silence.

My fingers twitch as I picture what Maaz must be doing at this moment. "She has duties in the ether, attending to Sadal," I say coldly.

I think back to the night we summoned him. When Maaz confessed her failure, he was furious. I have not seen Sadal often, but I have never seen him look so murderous. His eyes flashed dark and his lips settled into a cruel smile. He isn't the Dark One because he abhors punishment and anger. He welcomes them. Even now, he must be punishing her with his sick games.

I shudder. He likes to take disobedient Bloodbane into the ether when circumstances call for it. And there he will pretend to be kind, only to toss them into the void to meet with their truest self. It's enough to drive any Bloodbane mad.

When she asked him for armies to accomplish the task, he laughed in her face. Then Sadal beat her until she and I – nearly identical – could hardly be compared. At first, it was amusing as all beatings are. Then I grew bored. But as it continued and her shrieks fell silent, my own stomach was twisted and sick.

I blink as I come back to my sense. My companion is speaking. "Why not attack now?" She whines. "They're drunk and unguarded."

"Two witches against hundreds of noble Fae and Altair's guard?" I smirk. "Don't be a fool. We're formidable, but we're not invincible. So, unless you're looking to die tonight and broadcast to Altair's entire kingdom that we haven't finished with him, then be my guest."

Her lips twist into a frown. "Bitch." I hear her whisper under breath.

I chuckle. Maaz and I selected this young witch for grooming. We thought she had enough fire in her to lead the Bloodbane someday. Clearly, we were right. There aren't many Bloodbane that would dare speak to me with such insolence.

I cock my head as I spy a messenger running up the palace drive. "Look." I tilt my chin in his direction.

"So?" The witch sighs.

"A messenger on Summer's Eve," I say thoughtfully. "This is important."

"What do you want to do? Snatch him from the ground?" She asks, her attention snapping towards the messenger with renewed interest.

I drift lower. "Perhaps."

The messenger disappears into the palace and we hover near a tower, out of sight of the patrol. Maaz was never one for discretion, she has a flair for the dramatic. The Bloodbane have gotten used to following suit and I can tell that the witch beside me is itching to sweep directly into the castle. I hover in front of her, blocking her from doing just that. While Maaz works in the spotlight, I prefer to tug on the tangled webs in the shadows.

Soon enough, the messenger will leave, and we will interrogate him. Altair's guard is sparse tonight, no doubt because of the celebration. We will flit down into the light and back up into the darkness before anyone of the insolent Fae have noticed us.

While we wait, I take note of the castle defenses. The walls aren't even particularly high, and I see no defense weaponry whatsoever. I grin to myself, tugging my hood into place. Whatever army Sadal grants us will be more than enough to overrun this elegant palace. Light floods over the courtyard as the doors open. I spot the familiar shoulders of the messenger and swoop down without warning.

The young witch exclaims sharply but I silence her with a flick of my wrist. The Fae messenger turns just as I level out, his eyes widen, and his mouth goes slack as he takes in the wild-eyed Bloodbane swooping towards him. I have him in my arms, one hand wrapped around his mouth to silence him while I control my broom with the other. The rushing of the wind in my cloak and the surge of adrenaline from the hasty abduction are like a drug to me.

I return to the young witch and we take cover behind one of the gabled roofs of the palace. The messenger is quiet as I lift my hand away from his lips. He knows better than to scream when the Bloodbane have him in our grasp.

I smile pleasantly, tugging my hood back. His eyes rove over my supple breasts and full lips but he doesn't move. He's frozen like a mouse in a field.

"Tell us your message," the young witch demands.

I roll my eyes at her. "No," the messenger says stiffly.

I cradle the Fae man in one arm as I reach into my cloak for my dagger. The hilt is engraved with a phoenix and the blade is softly curved. I've had the dagger since I was a young girl, when my father gave it to me. It glistens in the starlight. I twist it in front of the Fae and sigh softly.

"It's coated in Oakswald. You know what that is, don't you?" He shudders in my arms. I grin. "One tiny slip of this blade against your skin, and you'll have thousands of microscopic parasites eating away at your flesh. It's not poison, it's much worse. First, they eat the meat and bones around the cut. But they don't work their way through you from there. Their favorite snack is right between your legs."

"What do you want?" He says hoarsely, clenching his legs together.

I smile, eyeing the young witch imperiously. "We want to know what you told our little Altair."

"What I told the King is none of your concern." His words are strong, but I can hear the fear in his voice.

I sigh loudly and slouch. "If you don't tell me, I won't hesitate to let my parasitic friends here delight themselves on your perfect, Fae flesh. You know perfectly well that we Bloodbane aren't the compassionate type."

He clenches his mouth tightly shut. I shrug and lower the blade to his leg. The sheen of the Oakswald on the blade is bright at this angle. I grin, even if he doesn't give me what I want, I'll certainly enjoy watching him waste away. They always writhe so powerfully they bite their own tongues off.

"Wait," the messenger blurts. "I'll tell you."

"Oh, good," I purr.

"General Kane discovered one of our border towers completely destroyed and the bodies disappeared. There were signs of a struggle, but no remains," the messenger says quickly, panting.

I purse my lips and meet the young witch's eyes, testing her. "Tell me what this means."

"Altair knows we're coming," she says, narrowing her eyes and staring out towards the mountains.

"It means one of our covens needs to be punished," I snap.

The messenger shifts against me. "Can I go?" He asks nervously.

I smile and tilt my head. "Of course."

With a flourish, I slip my blade over his knee, slicing through the thin layer of skin and flesh. He howls in pain and fear. Without touching the blood coating the blade or the residue of the Oakswald, I slip the dagger into its sheath. The Fae man is panting uncontrollably, clutching at his knee as his skin slowly disintegrates.

"They're eating rather quickly," I muse. "Must have been hungry."

"You said," he moans, trailing off.

I ease my broom away from the tower. "I lied."

Cackling, I release my hold on him and watch as he drops several stories to the cobblestone drive below. The young witch and I rocket away from the palace and back to the mountains. Maaz and Sadal must be told of what we've learned. Any suspicions from Altair could give him enough time to move against us before we've managed to secure our army. There is no time for games anymore. War is on the horizon.

CHAPTER 8

I take a long sip of wine as the Fae woman sighs dramatically. The wrinkles around the corners of her eyes deepen as she scowls. "I've never liked mortals," she quips. "I've always found them to be stupid and petty creatures. It's a pity that King Altair is forced to marry one because of the curse."

Irritation sparks in my chest, and I squeeze the flute of wine in my hand imperceptibly. Since Altair left me, Thal has been leading me through the calmer crowds of Fae, introducing me to nobles of significance. This woman has spent the last several minutes complaining loudly and often about mortals.

"He could kill me instead," I say, cocking a brow. "The curse would be just as broken as it is now."

The woman purses her thin lips. "Perhaps you think you're funny. Our King is a man of honor."

"I never said he wasn't." I finish off the wine and search for another.

Beside me, Thal already has one in hand. He exchanges my goblet for a new one with a flourish. "Watch yourself, mortal, Fae wine is strong," the older Fae woman warns me.

"I'm sure Thal will know when to cut me off." I smile sarcastically. "Until then, I will enjoy this delicious wine while the rest of the Fae participate in their giant orgy underneath that very arch."

"Savages. We Fae have long since outgrown those ancient rituals," she says.

"Not all, apparently." I raise my glass. "To willful and petty creatures."

The woman narrows her eyes at me, as if she senses the sarcasm dripping from my words. "You're the perfect example of why most Fae can't stand mortals. So young, and yet you think your cleverness is impressive. This is exactly why you don't belong on the throne. I could never stand for it."

I lower my glass, my eyes filled with quiet anger. "You could never stand for it? Could you have given up your life and family for one man?"

Without another word, I take a long drink of the wine and smack my lips together. She curls her lips in a deep frown but I only give her a simpering smile. I pivot and stomp through the crowd towards an empty corner for some peace. Navi has drifted off to make large sweeps through the crowd in a circle around me, leaving me with Thal.

"Do you know who that was?" He asks, chuckling low.

I eye him. "I'm sure introductions were made but I made a point of forgetting once she decided to insult all of humanity."

"Lady Reina Yointus; a very powerful family." Thal leans against the pillar beside me and smiles. "I fear you've just made an enemy."

"You don't look very afraid," I say bitingly.

"Oh, I'm more amused than anything – and impressed."

"Impressed?" I laugh mirthlessly. "I'm sure Altair will be anything but impressed."

Thal moves quickly, filled with deadly grace. He leans close to me, his breath brushing my ear. "Altair has grown much more serious, like an old man. A man like that could never please a woman like you."

"A woman like me?" I laugh, stepping out of arms reach as his fingers graze up my arm.

He isn't fazed by the distance I've put between us. Thal closes it in an instant. "Willful and childish." He grins.

I smirk and roll my eyes. For an instant, I almost thought he was serious. "Yes, those are very important qualities in a partner. Where is Altair?"

It's been almost an hour since he disappeared. My cheeks heat as I remember the passion we shared just before he rushed from the room. I don't know what got into me, letting him kiss me like that in front of a room filled with strangers. But for the first time in a long time, I felt wanted and needed, craved even. It was a heady feeling, and I gave into it. I felt like we might have a chance.

"Get your mind out of the gutter," Thal teases, pulling away finally.

I blush deeper and purse my lips. "Says the biggest playboy in all of Alnembra."

Thal shrugs. "Altair must have had to fulfill some of his kingly duties. It wouldn't take this long to calm from the fog of Summer's Eve."

"Why doesn't it affect you?" I ask, curiosity welling in me.

"I don't need Summer's Eve to give into my basest desires." He grins. "I do it all the time anyway."

"Charming," I say with a smirk. I turn towards the ballroom door to see if Altair may have returned. "Is he coming back?"

Thal looses a breath. "I'm sure he will try. In all truth, Verity, Altair can hardly stand to be apart from you."

My heart skips a beat. I don't know what I want anymore, but I can't deny the flush of happiness that blooms through me. "Still, he left me here," I say.

"He is the King," Thal says quietly. "It will be like this more often than you think. Altair will miss important moments with you to attend to his duties. He can't be everywhere at once."

I feel a twinge of irritation at Thal's condescending tone – as if I'm a child he needs to educate. "I'm not asking him to. But I won't deny I would like it if he could follow through with his commitment to take me to the ball."

"If you want a man like that, a king simply won't do." Thal clucks his tongue. "I, on the other hand, would be the perfect choice."

"Oh, really?" I laugh.

"Laugh all you want," Thal says smoothly. "But I can't be trusted with responsibility, which makes the perfect man for you. Think of all the time I'll have to shower you with affection."

"I've never heard such a pathetic attempt to woo a woman before in my life," Altair says from the shadows.

I jolt back, eyes wide with surprise as he melts out of the darkness. His hazel eyes are narrowed towards Thal, his hands balled into fists. Thal smiles broadly. "Cousin, you're back. Verity was just starting to miss you."

"Was she?" Altair eyes me.

"Clearly I can't be trusted to entertain a lady of her caliber for more than ten minutes," Thal jokes.

"Then, go," Altair murmurs.

A thrill courses through me at Altair's dangerous tone and the shadows in his eyes. I press my lips together, ducking my eyes as Altair and Thal face off. Thal's eyes flash but he dips his chin towards me. "Enjoy the evening, Verity."

I lift a hand to wave as he weaves through the crowd towards the naked, writhing Fae under the arch. I turn on Altair, frowning. "You didn't have to do that."

"You would rather spend the night with Thal?" Altair asks, finally stepping into the light.

"He was joking," I say, rolling my eyes. "He was only teasing me because I wanted you to return. He said you were likely working."

"I was," Altair quips.

My lips pull back into a frown as disappointment rushes through me. I had hoped that his long absence had nothing to do with business – that maybe he truly needed time to regain his senses. "What was so important that you couldn't stay at the ball with me?"

"The Bloodbane are attacking my borders," he says softly so no one will hear. "I was planning my next steps and sending messages to my generals."

"The Bloodbane," I say flatly. I'm tired of hearing about the Bloodbane. I'm tired of their childish bickering and the never-ending conflict. I exhale sharply through my nose.

"What?" He snaps.

"The Bloodbane couldn't have waited for one night? Not even one night – a few hours?" I scowl.

Altair presses his lips together impatiently. "I am a king, Verity. My country must come first."

"Of course," I sigh, defeated. "I'm tired."

"Tired?" Altair's voice is laced with disbelief. "Don't tell me you're ready to return to your rooms?"

My cold gaze slips towards him. "I am."

Altair rubs his temples, forcing his coifed hair out of place. "I shall escort you to your rooms."

"No," I quip, gathering my skirts. "Enjoy the Summer's Eve. Announce our engagement if you want."

"Verity," he growls, reaching for me.

I dance out of his reach. "Go be a king."

Without another word, I force my way through the crowds towards the ballroom doors. The Fae are drunk now, even the ones that have lingered on the sidelines throughout the night are feeling the call of their past. I wonder if Altair will join them tonight. I feel a flash of jealousy at the thought; imagining Altair with strange Fae women. I swallow, forcing every emotion but anger and disappointment away.

I slip through the ballroom doors, hoping that maybe Altair will be on my heels to convince me to stay. But he isn't. Pursing my lips, I kick the heels off my feet and walk barefoot through the castle halls towards my room. The castle seems empty now, all of the servants are either asleep or celebrating Summer's Eve elsewhere. My thoughts wander to Dain, the sly gardener. I wonder how he celebrates; if he's with a woman.

Summer's Eve was a disaster for me. But that seems to be the pattern here. I use my shoulder to push open my door and kick it shut with my foot. The fire is burning merrily, as it always is during the night. I slump into an armchair in front of it and let the flames warm my bare feet. My tulle skirts are bunched around my waist and wrinkling, but I don't care.

Already, I feel traces of regret pricking at me. I shouldn't have reacted so emotionally. I shouldn't have let it bother me that Altair chose to work over returning to me. What we have between us is unconventional and unpredictable. He is a king and I am his silly mortal fiancée. I sigh and lift my left hand to study the ring on my finger.

Perhaps it's time that I stopped fighting the inevitable.

CHAPTER 9

ALTAIR

I stare at Verity's lovely figure disappearing through the crowd. Her tulle skirts are almost caught in the ballroom door as she slips through it. She's gone. I growl, hands clenched into fists at my side. I was gone longer than I intended, but the situation with the Bloodbane couldn't be ignore. I rub my temples. Why can't Verity understand that?

I hear footsteps approach, Thal's light but sure steps. I turn my head, eyes narrowing towards him. "Thal," I snarl.

He purses his lips. "I crossed a line."

"Damn right you did," I say roughly. "That is my future wife."

"And she's unhappy," he snaps. His green eyes flash and I feel a surge of hesitation.

"What do you care if she's unhappy?" I ask, my tone softening.

Thal glances away, his shoulders stiffening. "Verity is a good woman. She deserves to be happy. As do you, cousin."

He turns away before I can respond, and I feel as if I've been doused with cold water. Is it me that's making Verity unhappy? Am I a more terrible beast than I was before she saved me? My heart clenches painfully in my chest and I scowl. This is not how

I anticipated this night. I had imagined that the ball would be the perfect chance for Verity and I to grow closer, to enjoy each other's company.

"Altair," Navi says from behind me.

I turn and loose a sigh. "What is it?"

Navi wraps a hand around the hilt of her sword and purses her full lips. She shakes out her short hair. "It's good that Verity retired for the night. The moon is full now, and your guests are getting wilder by the minute."

I snort softly at Navi's attempts to console me. She's thoughtful and observant, but not always empathetic. "Thank you, Navi," I say. "I think I'll go as well."

She nods sharply and strides away, ever resilient of her duty. I rake a hand through my dark hair and sigh. I had hoped that after Verity broke the curse, we would find happiness. I would find happiness. But it evades me still.

I unbutton my jacket around the collar and sigh as I stride towards the ballroom door. No one will miss me now that the festivities have taken a raucous turn. I'm not interested in celebrating with my subjects. The only one I wanted to be with tonight was Verity, and for an instant, I was.

In the hall, I turn towards the stairs where Verity would have gone. Maybe I can still salvage this night, maybe I can find her and make it right. My gaze drops to the floor. I can never make it right. My time will always be split unevenly between her and my duties. And if she can't learn to forgive me for it, then we can never be happy together. The thought almost makes me sick to my stomach.

Suddenly, I hear running footsteps approaching. I turn, alert, to see a foot soldier sprinting towards me. He skids to a halt in front of me, panting. "Your Grace, there's been a murder."

"Show me," I demand.

He turns back and hurries the way he came. I follow, taking one last look over my shoulder in the direction of Verity's room.

But I have work to do. Work that never seems to end. The foot soldier leads me out the main doors and down the steps. At the bottom of the stairs, I see a cluster of guards and a few healers. They part silently for me and my stomach recoils as I see what captured their attention.

The messenger that left me only a little while ago is crumbled and folded on the cobblestones. Blood pools around him and coats his face and limbs. I see bones protruding from his skin at odd angles, jagged and streaked in blood. It looks as if he fell from a great height. Lips twisted with disgust and regret, I glance up. There are no parapets here, only open sky.

"What happened here?" I ask.

One of the healers clears their throat. "It appears that he fell."

"From where?" I demand.

Everyone exchanges a glance. "We don't know."

I turn away from the sky and back to the messenger. I was going to send him back to my generals once I finished my letters, but I never did find him. Now I know why. "Take care of this," I say quietly. "Prepare his body for the funeral and send word to his family with my regards."

"Yes, Your Majesty," a guard says.

The soldiers lift his corpse gingerly and follow the healers into the bowels of the castle where they embalm those who die inside my walls. I look to the sky once more. The stars wink brightly, as if nothing in the world is wrong. Suddenly, a star disappears before shining again. And another. I narrow my eyes, straining to see. My heart drops as I catch a glimpse of a red cloak flickering in the light of the moon.

Two Bloodbane witches soar above me, heading for the mountains. One of their hoods slips away and I recognize the pale blond hair of its rider. Maaz. My hands clench into fists at my side as I realize what they've done to the messenger. They killed him because he gave me news of the border tower. And now they know that I know of their movements. They know they've lost the element of surprise and I've lost the slight advantage I had over them.

They'll fly back to their mountain keep and strategize. The Bloodbane will be moving quickly now. I need to move even faster. I crouch and change into the form I wore while I was cursed. My limbs stretch and bulge with muscles, my fingernails curl into heavy claws. I feel my face morph into that of a jaguar, hair sprouting over me. My vision sharpens and brightens in the dark. I stretch out my wings, flexing them. It's been weeks since I last wore this form. After Verity broke the curse, I thought I didn't want anything to do with the familiar beast. But I've missed it.

With a single beat of my wings, I launch myself into the night sky. I stretch my wings as they catch the air and buoy me higher. I don't know how I kept the ability to wear this form after Verity broke the curse, but it seems only fitting that now I can use it against Maaz.

I soar through the night sky towards the ruins of the border tower. The castle falls away from my sight. I fly over a few scattered villages. Bonfires roar in the town squares as the Fae dance around the flames. When I was young, Thal and I would sneak out on Summer's Eve and visit the nearest villages to celebrate with the common folk. Now, it hardly seems familiar.

Soon enough, the forest stretches out beneath me, thick and dense. There are no villages this deep into the forest and few roads cut through it. It's the perfect place for the Bloodbane to launch an attack against me without catching my attention. I swoop lower as I approach the location of the border tower.

Instead of a tall, stone tower that stands above the trees, the space is empty. I circle the ruins, taking in the huge stone boulders that now rest on the ground. The tower has been scattered, the trees around it crushed by the giant stones that fell from it. The Bloodbane used some sort of powerful magic or catapults to fell the tower. I drop onto the stones and sniff. I smell no animals, no Fae, and no Bloodbane. All I smell is the strong scent of foul magic.

With a growl, I pick through the rubble, looking for any signs that the Bloodbane or my soldiers may have left behind. But the rubble is only filled with stone, dirt, broken furniture, and scattered weapons.

The soldiers stationed here were caught by surprise and slaughtered. What the Bloodbane have done with their bodies, I can't imagine. But the Bloodbane don't take Fae prisoners, they detest us too much for that. I take a final look around the devastated tower before flying back to the castle.

When I touch down onto the tallest tower, the sun is already peeking over the horizon. Birds herald the dawn with their singing. Below me, the festivities are coming to an end, but it will be another hour or so before my guests stagger out of the castle and back to their homes.

With a sigh, I lay down on the cold stones of the tower, staring to the east to watch the sun rise. A gentle wind rustles my feathers. Deja-vu settles in me with a feeling of melancholy. I miss the days during the curse that I had nothing to rule over and no duties to fulfill besides trying to make Verity fall in love with me. Now, even my nights are spent working, while Verity suffers alone.

I roll onto my back, careful not to crush my wings. I wonder if I will ever be satisfied. I have thousands of years to live and I want to be content. I want the woman beside me to be happy. I want Alnembra to be safe and prosperous. But that can never be as long as the Bloodbane continue to target Alnembra for their mysterious purpose. The balancing act is taking its toll.

I picture Verity in her room, sleeping soundly. She has no idea what I do to keep this country safe, no idea of the fears that plague me. I growl softly to myself, anger flaring within me. She complains of my absence, but if she had any idea what we truly faced, perhaps she would think differently. My gaze softens and I feel a wave of guilt at my anger towards her. I don't want Verity to know of the horrors that the Bloodbane will inflict upon us if we can't stop them.

I crawl to my feet and slip over the edge of the tower. I stretch my wings, catching air to buoy me up. Lazily, I soar towards Verity's room. The windows and balcony are dark, the only light inside the fading fire. I perch on the balcony railing and peer inside. Verity is curled on her bed, still dressed in the tulle gown. I smile internally, taking in her peaceful face.

Suddenly, my stomach drops as I see a shadow looming over her. The stone railing cracks and crumbles as my claws tighten around it. I lean forward, a snarl rumbling in my chest. The shadow stretches out, like a hand, and caresses her cheek. The sun peeks over the mountains, shining into Verity's room. As the room brightens, the shadow disappears as quickly as it came. My eyes narrow as I try to pierce the details and corners of her room, searching for any sign of it. But there's nothing. But I know what I saw.

CHAPTER 10

The scent of old paper perfumes the air and I breathe it in deeply. I love that smell. It reminds me of when I was a girl and I devoured every book I could get my hands on. I became a librarian because of my childhood spent reading and living in my fantasy worlds. Now, I have the library of my dreams at my disposal, but I don't feel any satisfaction.

Sighing, I pick through the shelves, searching for anything that might relate to the Bloodbane witches. I need to learn more about myself and my history. Ever since I broke the curse, I've had this feeling – this nagging sensation that there is more to me than I want to admit. I want to find out what.

The wizened librarian rounds the corner. Her Fae ears are pointed, and her stride is strong, but wrinkles line her eyes and mouth. She's older than Reina Yointus even. She lifts her eyes from the cart of books she pushes and smiles. I've never learned her name, and I doubt the librarian will ever tell me. She seems to enjoy living in anonymity, watching from the sidelines.

"I haven't forgotten that you agreed to teach me how to tend for this library," I say as she approaches.

"And yet you never come to learn." She stops the cart beside me and slips a heavy tome onto the shelf.

I purse my lips. "I'm sorry, I have other things on my mind."

"Help yourself to our shelves, but I'm afraid you won't find what you're searching for here," she says, her voice deep with warning.

"What do you mean?" I ask, furrowing my brows.

"I told you, we don't keep many books about the Bloodbane here. The answers you seek aren't in any of our records," she says as she begins to push her cart away.

I jog after her. "Why not?"

I never asked about the animosity between them; how it started and why. I don't know how long the Bloodbane have plagued the Fae, or if the Fae started it all. I only know that Altair and his people want nothing to do with the witches in the mountain. And if they knew how close I feel to the Bloodbane, they would want nothing to do with me.

"The Fae and the Bloodbane witches have been enemies for thousands of years. King Alshain had many of our records that contained information about their magic destroyed as a precaution," she explains.

"King Alshain?" I pull my lips into a confused frown.

"King Altair's father," the librarian says softly.

Altair's father. He's never told me his name and I've never seen portraits of him or the Queen anywhere in the castle. I wonder if Altair tries to forget them. "Why would he do that?" I muse.

The librarian shrugs and trundles away. The squeaking of her cart's wheels fade, and I'm left alone in silence again. I bite my lip, wishing someone would leave me with more answers than questions. But the doesn't seem to be he way of the Fae. If I can't find the answers I need in Altair's library, I don't know where else to look. A memory of the library in Desmarais flashes through my mind and I feel a spark of hope. But it disappears when I remember that not even Altair can access their records. That library is sealed.

With a huff of frustration, I carry what books I have managed to find back towards the sitting area. I used to read in front of the floor to ceiling window. It made me feel special when Altair would fly by to check on me. Now, I don't want him or anyone watching me. So, I read in the corner where I dragged a comfortable arm chair. It strains my eyes to read in the dimmer light, but it's worth it to have my privacy.

I round the corner, turning away from the light-filled lounge and towards my dark corner. My heart stops as I notice that someone has dragged a chair in front of mine and is sitting with his back to me. My stomach turns as I take in the dark hair. I come here for solace and privacy, yet Altair has sent another soldier to keep an eye on me like a child.

I exhale sharply through my nose, and I know the Fae has heard my frustration. I want him to know. I want him to leave me alone. I sit stiffly in the chair, setting my books aside before turning to the soldier. My eyes widen as I realize that this is no soldier; it's Dain.

He smiles, his dark eyes intense. "Hello, Verity."

"Dain," I say, blushing. "What are you doing here?"

"I wanted to see you again," he says simply. "I know how much you love the library, so I thought I would find you here."

I look around at the massive room. You could be searching for a person all day and never find them. "How did you know I would be here? In this chair?"

"It seems like you're in need of privacy," he says simply. "I guessed."

"Good guess," I mutter. I turn to him, suddenly worried. "You shouldn't be here. If Altair sees you, or finds out from one of his guards –"

"I'll deal with that when the time comes," he cuts me off.

I chew my bottom lip. I don't miss the way his eyes settle on my lips hungrily. "How was your Summer's Eve?"

"Pleasant," he says with a grin. "Very pleasant."

I've seen that same grin on human men who've slept with a beautiful woman. "Who is she? A lover?" I ask, pretending to be disinterested. I study my stack of books while I wait for him to reply.

"Something like that," he says. "But I couldn't get you off my mind."

My heart beats faster at his words and I feel a flush wash through me. "Dain," I say, my voice laced with warning.

I can't continue down this path. I can't let my body heat with desire or give in to the man who makes his interest in me clear. Even if Altair has set me by the wayside, I'm still committed to him.

Dain smiles, but his eyes are sharp. I feel a spark of curiosity while I stare at him. At first glance, he's a normal Fae man. But there's some intelligence in his eyes that's dangerous, and very magnetic. He leans forward, his fingers tracing my knee. I don't move to stop him, even though every cell in my body is screaming at me that this simple acceptance is betraying Altair. Dain's smile broadens.

"I have a gift for you," he says.

"A gift?" I echo, lost in the tingling sensation of his fingers on my skin. Even through the fabric of my trousers, I can feel his heat.

"That's why I'm really here," he explains. He pulls away from me, leaving me aching internally. I watch as he draws a heavy text out of his satchel on the floor. He offers the book to me.

"What is it?" I ask, taking it. The book is bound in black leather with red detailing. The engraved details have faded, and I can't tell if they were once vines wrapping around the frame of the book, or curtains of blood.

Dain leans forward again, his hands finding me. I shudder pleasantly. "Open it," he whispers.

I flip to a random page in the middle of the huge text and I feel my blood sing. Bloodbane magic. Bloodbane rituals. I look up breathlessly. "Where did you get this?"

Dain's hands massage my knees, and he smiles. "Don't worry about where I found it; it's yours now. I want you to find the answers to your questions."

"Why?" I ask, my fingers clenched tightly around the leather binding.

"I want you to be happy," he says sharply. "It's clear you aren't happy and that you're searching for answers Altair and the other Fae refuse to give you. I want to help. I want you to know who you are if that will help you find peace."

"Dain," I murmur, dropping my gaze back to the book. "Thank you."

His eyes glimmer, so dark even his irises look black. "This text can only tell you so much. You would find all the answers to your questions if you went directly to the Bloodbane or spoke to Sadal Melik."

My stomach turns at his words. "The Bloodbane will kill me," I say. "And I don't want to speak to Sadal, I don't want to covenant with him."

"Why are you so afraid of him?" Dain asks, his brows furrowed with confusion.

The questions spins around through my mind. Why don't I want to meet with Sadal? Why am I apprehensive? I shake my head, trying to clear my mind. "He's cruel," I finally say.

"Sometimes you have to be cruel to be kind," Dain says softly. "It's your choice. I simply want you to find peace, peace that even Altair can't give you."

My heart swells at Dain's kind words, at the gentle smile he offers me. Altair has always told me he wants me to be happy, he tries to find ways to please me. But Dain has actually listened. He's giving me what I need. "Thank you, Dain," I whisper.

He stands and bends over me. My heart beats wildly, blood pumping faster as anticipation flits through me. I feel a rush of adrenaline as his face hovers only inches from mine. He doesn't move any closer, doesn't drop his lips to mine like I suddenly crave. My breath is short and rushed, and I know he can hear it with his Fae hearing. He doesn't smirk like Altair does when he sees how I'm reacting to him.

Dain smiles kindly and trails his fingers over my cheek. I lean into his touch without thinking, my eyes hooded. "Find me in the gardens whenever you need me, Verity," he murmurs. "For anything at all."

"Verity?" I hear Altair's voice echo towards me.

I jolt, and blink rapidly as if being drawn from a mind fog. My heart clenches in fear as I realize Altair will find me with Dain. Altair rounds the corner, his footsteps sharp on the stone floor. I straighten my back and meet his gaze defiantly; I'll stand up for Dain if Altair says anything. Altair stops a few feet from me and looks curiously at me.

"Why are there two chairs?" He asks, eyes narrowing.

My lips part in surprise and I resist twisting around to see if Dain is behind me. I chew the inside of my cheek. "To put my feet up," I lie.

Altair cocks his head and then glances around. I stuff the book on Bloodbane magic behind my stack of texts, so he won't see it. Altair purses his lips but seems satisfied that we're alone. He sits stiffly in the armchair across from me. I twist, pretending to be stretching my back as I search for Dain. Dain is nowhere to be seen. He must have melted into the shadows and slipped between the bookshelves while I was panicking about Altair.

I sigh in relief and turn back to Altair. "What are you doing here? Don't you have meetings?"

"Hello to you too," he says, cocking a brow.

I roll my eyes. "Hello, Altair."

"Did you miss me?" He asks teasingly, his eyes glittering playfully.

"No," I quip. He breaks into a smile. Altair knows I haven't forgotten our fight last night on Summer's Eve.

"I didn't think so," he says. His voice is light, but his eyes are dark. "I came to apologize."

I cock a brow. Altair isn't the type to apologize. "Apologize?"

"I shouldn't have left you alone during Summer's Eve for so long," Altair sighs and rakes a hand through his dark hair. "I'm not good at finding a balance between my duties. There are so many things that only I can fix, so many threats and worries." His voice is heavy and he pauses for a moment. "But I haven't made you a priority. I'm grateful to you for what you've sacrificed for me and Alnembra, and what you will continue to sacrifice. I will work harder."

His voice is heavy and tired. I bite my lip, realizing just how heavy the burden on Altair must be. I feel a rush of guilt at my own selfishness. "Is there anything I can do to help?" I ask, brows twitching together.

"There is," he says. His tone is still serious, and I miss the light, teasing version of Altair I grew to know.

"What is it?" I ask. I don't want to make his burdens heavier. I want to help.

"We need to make wedding preparations," he says softly.

I blanch. "When?"

"Now," Altair says. "We need to decide when to be married and then begin our preparations."

"So soon?" I ask, toying with the ring on my finger.

"I thought you wanted to help?" Altair's voice is cold.

I glance up, catching his chilly gaze. My muscles go stiff as I feel a wave of frustration. "I do. Just forget it."

"No, Verity." Altair leans forward and splays his hands. "Tell me, what could be so terrible about marriage to me that you want to postpone our wedding?"

I narrow my eyes at him, trying to keep my frustration out of my voice. "I was nearly married all of a month ago, and now you're asking me to marry you. Can you understand that I'm apprehensive?"

"No," he says sharply. "I can't, because you made this choice knowingly."

"Not completely," I protest, brows furrowing.

His sits back commandingly. "We will be married within the next four weeks, pick a date soon."

I jump to my feet as he rises. He smooths out his tunic and eyes me as I fume. "You aren't my king," I hiss.

Altair purses his lips and stares at me coldly. "I'm curious, Verity, why you broke the curse at all if you can't be bothered to follow through."

Without waiting for my response, he turns away. I watch his strong back as he strides towards the library doors. They slam shut behind him, leaving me glaring. I grind my teeth together and throw myself back into the armchair. Part of me hopes that Dain heard the whole thing and that he'll return. But I'm not some damsel in distress who needs a harem of men and lovers, I remind myself. I'm Verity Chastain, part Bloodbane witch, I think forcefully. I don't need anyone. I bite the inside of my cheek angrily until I draw blood.

I swallow the tangy liquid. I thought for a moment that Altair and I could reconcile with each other. I believe he is sorry that his duties as King have left him little time for me. He's left me feeling more like a prisoner now than I did before I saved him. He knows this, he regrets it. And yet he still treats me like I'm his hostage.

I reach for the Bloodbane text and open to the first page. I'm not Altair's. I'm not Sadal's. I am my own. I'll find out who I am even if Altair tries to stop me. I'm a Bloodbane witch, or at least as close to one as a human can be. And I won't be toyed with by anyone, let alone my future husband. Perhaps when I've finally learned of my history and my potential, Altair will take me more seriously. But by then, perhaps I won't care about him at all.

By then, perhaps I'll be free.

CHAPTER 11

The frozen wind howls through the mountain peaks, stinging my sharp cheeks. My red cloak snaps against me, the hood falling away from my face. Beside me, Maaz stares out over the mountain crags and gullies with anticipation. I turn away from her, towards the pitch-black shadows in the crannies of the mountain range below us.

The keep is quiet tonight. I warned the leaders of our covens to keep our sisters inside while Maaz and I waited for the gift Sadal promised us. The gift he promised her. I press my lips into a thin line, thinking of the way I found her when I returned on Summer's Eve. Maaz was bloodied and broken in the Holy Rite. She had emerged from the ether before I returned and curled herself up in the bottom of the well, tears dried on her face.

Sadal had taken his time toying with her. Time in the ether isn't linear; past, present, and future collide until time itself feels like a trap. Everything grows muddled in the ether, which makes it twice as maddening as it would be otherwise. My sister endured no torture, while surviving hundreds of years of pain at the same time.

I healed her, though it took a few days. Now, she waits eagerly for Sadal to return to her, as if he never struck her at all. I bite the inside of my cheek, drawing blood. I warned her not to trust him. I warned her to leave him out of this and let him enjoy the conquest when it was over. But she didn't listen. As the leader of the Bloodbane, Sadal will punish her for every mistake we make.

"I see it," she whispers breathlessly. Her fingers dig into the stone railing of the balcony.

I peer into the black beneath us. "There's nothing there, Maaz."

"Look," she hisses, pointing.

I follow her finger, trying to discern anything in the murky darkness. Suddenly, I see the shadows coiling like black smoke. The darkness moves, as if it were a heavy fog, disturbed by some unseen wind. I swallow thickly, heart pumping wildly. For thousands of years, the creatures of darkness have been trapped in the ether, waiting for the day they could return to the physical world. Now that Maaz has extended an invitation, the portals hidden in the depths of these mountains have been opened.

A harsh scream shatters the silence, echoing through the mountains. A chill slips down my spine and my grip tightens around the balcony. The scream is followed by a chorus of unearthly screeches and fear lances through me. The Bloodbane have been the most feared worshippers of darkness in this realm, but now the Fae will have something else to fear. Something far worse. Something even I fear.

Out of the shadows, black creatures erupt. They scale the mountainside, crawling on all fours like animals. I take a step back on instinct, my heart pounding fearfully in my chest. Maaz simply smiles. She turns to me, her pale blue eyes bright with excitement. "Aren't they beautiful, Cleo?"

My lips twist into disbelief. The creatures are too far to discern details of their features. But I've heard enough myths to know that their skin is covered in black scales. Their claws are as long as my forearm, and their eyes are as yellow as their fangs. They carry the figure of men but are nothing like them. They move like beasts; they sound like predators. They're demons brought from the depths of the ether to tear apart any living creature that crosses their path.

"How will we control them?" I ask, my voice tight with worry. "How will we ensure that they don't raze the world to the ground and leave us with nothing?"

Maaz eyes me, her lips curled with rebuke. "Nothing they conquer for us will be ours, Cleo. It is for the Dark One."

"Will the Dark One live in solitude while there is nothing left for us to survive?" I snap.

Maaz turns away, ignoring my reply. She sighs, watching as the black horde scrambles over the mountain like flies on a carcass. "We will take Alnembra, and then we'll take the world," she says.

"So, they are to your liking?" Sadal asks, his silky voice floating from the shadows on the balcony.

Maaz turns towards his voice and bows her head reverently. "Master," she murmurs. "They are more magnificent than I dared dream."

I bite my tongue, resisting the urge to scream at him for what he did to my sister. Instead, I stare at him with narrowed eyes, listening to the chorus of howling demons behind me.

"Cleo?" Sadal asks, melting out of the shadows. "You're quiet."

I meet his dark gaze. Sadal's ivory skin almost glows in the dark of night, his black eyes filled with danger. He leans against the wall, cocking a brow. I dip my head in a shallow display of insincere reverence. "They look formidable, Dark One," I say stiffly.

"They are." He smiles wickedly. "One can shred through three Fae soldiers in seconds."

Sadal moves to Maaz's side and slips a lean arm around her waist. She leans into him, her eyes hazy with desire. I turn away and pretend to study the masses of demons at our doorstep. I was the first to give myself to Sadal, and she followed my footsteps. In the many years since, she devoted herself wholly to his dark enterprises. But her devotion to him sickens me.

"You know this doesn't come without a price," Sadal says, his fingers digging into Maaz's side.

My stomach drops like a stone and I turn my head slightly, eyes slipping towards them. "Did she not already pay the price?" I ask coldly. "Years of torture in the ether isn't enough for this army?"

"Consider it a first payment." Sadal smiles at me, studying me. "Now I require the second."

"Tell me, Master, and it will be done," Maaz says. She turns towards him, her hands on his chest.

Sadal's black eyes glimmer. "I want the walls of the keep soaked in blood."

"Whose blood?" I ask before Maaz can make any promises. The Dark One's requests are often laced with hidden punishment.

His eyes dart towards the door leading into the keep. "An entire Bloodbane coven."

My mouth falls slack and my heart stops in my chest. The Bloodbane are loyal on only two accounts; to Sadal and to ourselves. To kill an entire coven, dozens of witches, in return for an army of creatures from the darkness is impossible. My stomach churns at the thought.

"No," I say softly. "It can't be done. It won't be done. Each of these witches has given herself to you already; you own us. How can you ask for our blood?"

"Silence, Cleo," Maaz hisses. She swats at me, raking her fingernails over my cheek.

I snarl as my cheek stings and hot blood drips from the scratches. "These are our sisters."

Maaz glowers at me. "We all belong to our Master. He can do what he wishes with us. And we will follow his every command."

"Maaz," I say warningly.

"Dark One," Maaz says, turning back to Sadal. "Which coven do you desire?"

Sadal makes a show of deciding, stroking his clean-shaven chin with his hand. "The youngest. These dark creatures prefer young blood, it's sweeter."

I pale as Maaz turns to me. "Find Hamala's coven and bring them to the Holy Rite," she demands.

I stumble from the balcony as Maaz wraps herself in Sadal's embrace. The youngest coven has a girl, only sixteen years of age. She joined us only a month ago after escaping her cruel father. We promised her an eternity of pleasure and power. Now, she'll be dead; ripped apart by the foot-long claws of demons. Cold washes through me, turning my blood to ice in my veins.

Every cell in my body screams at me to turn back as I stride through the halls. Bile rises in my throat but I swallow it, eyes hard. I have a duty. I spent years working in the shadows, doing Maaz's bidding. Years of building my influence and power until it rivaled Maaz herself. I won't risk it all now.

I find Hamala and her coven in the great hall and I lead them to the Holy Rite wordlessly. As the youngest coven leader, Hamala knows not to question me. She's always been obedient and loyal to Maaz's leadership. As I close the great doors of the Holy Rite and lock them in, I sense her trepidation. The large, circular room is filled with blood-red cloaks. The witches cluster around the well, exchanging curious glances.

I wait on the sidelines, knowing Sadal and Maaz will join us soon. Sadal appears on my left, smirking. The young witches gasp at his sudden presence. The air feels electrified, charged with excitement at the sight of our Master. I cross my arms and drop back a few feet until I'm lingering in the shadows.

Sadal spreads his arms wide. "Die," he says, his powerful voice shaking the room.

I curl back into the wall as demons shatter through the balcony doors and fall upon the witches. They scream, shrieks of terror as the beasts tear through them. Bones crunch and the sound of squelching bodies fills the room. And over it all, the growling of the creatures. In seconds, blood pools around my feet, soaking my boots.

Sadal turns to me, smiling pleasantly. Behind him, the demons turn their yellow gaze on me in unison. I curl my hands into fists at my side, resisting the urge to reach for the dagger at my waist. It wouldn't do any good if Sadal made me their next meal.

"Cleo," Sadal croons. "I've always admired your stubborn and skeptical nature. I expected more of a fight from you."

"Is that what you wanted?" I ask softly, my eyes raking over what's left of the bodies.

"No." He shakes his head. "I have big plans for you. You must be careful not to disappoint me."

I eye the demons at his back, knowing that Sadal is deadlier than all of them combined. Maaz shoves her way through the scaled creatures to stand at his side. She smirks at me, blood splattered on the silk dress she wears beneath her cloak. I see blood stains on her hands, and I know she joined the fray.

I swallow my fury as the two of them tower over me. "I have someone I want you to meet," Sadal says.

A hulking demon stomps from the balcony towards us. He walks on two legs, his overly-long arms scraping the bloodied stones. His fangs are like tusks, extending over his lips. He turns his yellow eyes on me. "Zox," the creature growls.

"This is Zox," Sadal says pleasantly. "He leads the horde."

"Zox," the creature confirms.

Maaz looks delighted, staring up at the mammoth demon with bright eyes. "Impressive."

"Zox will take the horde across the borders and into the

villages and cities," Sadal explains. "He and the horde will leave the land soaking in Fae blood."

Maaz shivers, a smile tugging at her lips. "I can't wait."

"Altair will no doubt surrender," I say, my voice empty of feeling.

"He might, but that won't stop the horde," Sadal chuckles.

My stomach twists. I had expected as much. Zox roars, sending his demons loping out of the Holy Rite and down the keep walls. Sadal and Maaz wander away, whispering back and forth. I stare at the Holy Rite. The sacred room is littered with the bodies of my sisters, blood congealing between the stones. I wonder if soon the whole world will look this way.

CHAPTER 12

Candlelight flickers in Altair's private dining chambers. It's a familiar scenario; a quiet, unpleasant dinner with Altair. Just like the old days. He eyes me from across the table. His beard is growing back, just a soft shadow against his cheeks and strong jaw. I study him with empty eyes. Once, my heart would have fluttered seeing how handsome he is, but I have something else on my mind now.

The book Dain gave me is hidden in my room. I stuffed it behind one of the bookcases so none of the Fae will find it. I've read almost half of it now, reading almost constantly for two days. Normally, with a book of that size, I would be finished with it. But, somehow, even when I read for hours, I find myself staring at the same page.

"Is dinner to your liking?" Altair asks, clearing his throat.

I poke my knife against the succulent steak. "Stooping to small talk, Altair? That isn't like you."

He purses his lips, his eyes glinting with amusement. "There she is. I was wondering where Verity was hiding inside that beautiful body."

"What?" I narrow my eyes.

Altair leans forward, pushing his dinner aside. "I don't know what's on your mind lately, Verity, but it's becoming very clear that you are not yourself. I find tiny glimpses of you, as I did just now. But you've hidden yourself away. Why?"

"I don't know what you're talking about," I say. I feel a flush of heat creep to my cheeks and my stomach coils tightly. A few weeks ago, I might have been flattered that Altair is so keenly watching me, but now, it only makes me irate.

"What are you doing, Verity? Why are you so intent on pulling away from me?" He continues. His eyes, usually serious while he works or filled with mirth when he teases me, are dark and gloomy.

"Has it ever occurred to you that I am not pulling away? But that you are forcing this distance?" I snap. If he had simply let me be who I am, perhaps we wouldn't be in this mess.

"I haven't pushed you away, I'm trying to draw you in." He gestures, clenching his fists and tugging them to his chest.

I grit my teeth. "You don't understand."

"Help me understand," he whispers.

My thoughts flash back to the book hidden in my room. I feel a chill settle over my heart and I calm instantly. I drop my cutlery and push away from the table. I don't want to be here. I want to study the Bloodbane book. Altair rises as I do and is around the table in a flash. His face hovers inches from mine, his eyes searching my face.

"What?" I ask blandly.

"Verity," he murmurs. "Please, help me."

"I can't," I say simply. "I can't help you anymore. I've done enough."

I pull away from him, hardly noticing that his fingers brush against my arm pleadingly. Navi is in front of the door, staring at me coldly. She blocks my path, and I loose a breath through my nose. "The King hasn't dismissed you," she says coolly.

"He's not my king." I cock a brow. "I have no king."

"As long as you reside in this realm, he is your king," Navi says. Her hand strays to her sword.

"Let her go, Navi," Altair says from behind me.

"Altair," Navi say, her brows furrowed with confusion.

"Let her go." Altair's voice is laced with defeat.

"Yes, little dog, let me go," I quip, a smile tugging at my lips.

Navi's lips twist into a scowl and she moves aside swiftly. I toss her a cold smile before sweeping through the door. I hear her hiss in response, but the door is closing already. When the door has clicked shut, I walk swiftly towards my room. The book is calling my name, my blood singing in response.

I close the door to my room and rush to the bookcase. Grunting, I manage to slip the book from its recess. Its warm in my hands, as if its been waiting for me. My heart is beating quickly as I flip it open. I run my fingertips over the soft page, trailing the harshly written words. I have a lot to learn still. But Altair could find me here any minute. And if he chooses, he could send Navi after me. She would gladly cut me down if she found me reading this.

I wrap myself in a heavy cloak and hide the book in its folds. Quietly, I ease the door open and peek into the hall. It's empty. I hurry down the halls to the doors leading into the gardens. There's a candle in my pocket, along with a bundle of matches. The gardens are always empty at night. If I find a quiet corner to read, no one will find me until morning. Smiling softly, I walk purposefully through the hedge maze towards the overgrown trees near the back wall of the palace.

The trees are thick, their branches long and gnarled. They're bowed over with the weight of the leaves and fruit they bear, a clear marker that this part of the gardens will give me the solitude I seek. I duck beneath one of the overgrown branches and weave between the tall trunks until I find a bench covered in ivy and moss.

I sit, and light the candle I brought with me. Its yellow light flickers merrily in the small clearing, lighting up the trunks and foliage the protect me from sight. It's like a cave of green and living things. I perch the candle on the edge of the bench and open the cover of the Bloodbane book. A soft wind blows through my sanctuary, rustling the pages.

"Hello, Verity," Dain says.

I gasp, glancing up sharply for the source of his voice. I see him then, melting out of the shadows. He smiles, his eyes glimmering in the candlelight. "Dain," I sigh. "You scared me."

His smile broadens. "I'm sorry."

"What are you doing out here?" I ask suspiciously.

"I could ask you the same thing," he says, draping himself over the bench beside me. "I wanted to see you."

"You followed me," I say flatly.

Dain drops his gaze, ashamed. "I'm sorry. I saw you leave the castle. Two days without seeing you feels like eternity."

My heart pounds loudly at his words. "For a Fae, that sounds like torture."

"It is," he murmurs. "Forgive me."

"There's nothing to forgive." I shrug and turn back to the book. "Have you ever read this?" I ask, stroking the pages.

"Many times," he says. He loops an arm over the back of the bench, almost around my shoulders. "Shall we read it together?"

I nod breathlessly and shift the book closer to him. But Dain stops me, instead closing the distance between us. My hip and thigh are pressed against his, his arm holding me close. I can hardly breathe as he drops his head to my shoulder and nuzzles me. My body feels as if its on fire, electrified by a hundred volts. It's been too long since I felt this sort of attraction, the kind that instantly sets my blood pumping and my body aching. I sag into him unconsciously, sighing.

Silently, our eyes rove the pages, drinking in the words as one. As the hours pass, I catch myself leaning over the books as if I'm going to dive into it. Dain always draws me back with a soft stroke of his hands on my back. He's so gentle, so thoughtful. I lean into him, letting my eyes drift away from the text.

His hand strokes my arm and I turn towards him, feeling light-headed. "How do you find the book?" Dain asks, his voice soft and melodic. "Is it answering your questions?"

On the contrary, it's giving me more. I keep reading different spells and rituals, different beliefs of the Bloodbane. But I don't know how any of it relates to me. I don't know how to find myself in it, except that it feels right. I shake my head. "The more I read it, the more different I feel; as if I'm not myself anymore," I confess. "The more I learn, the more distant I grow from Altair."

"Why does that matter?" He asks in dulcet tones. His hand cups my cheek.

Why does it matter? My mind is foggy, filled with sparks and urges and desires that all lead to Dain. "I don't know," I breathe, my eyes locked on his.

Dain smiles softly, gently. And then his full lips are on mine. The kiss isn't gentle, the way I imagined it would be. Dain kisses me hard, his lips commanding me to surrender to him. He bites me roughly, pain lancing through me. But the pain sends a thrill of excitement through me. I rake my fingers through his dark hair, tangling them in it in a desperate attempt to get closer to him. I want to give myself to him, every cell in my body craves it. But there's a tickling reminder in the back of my mind that I belong to another man.

So, I crawl into his lap, straddling his hips, but I don't let him tear my silk dress away like I want him to. Dain's hands grip my hips, moving me against him. I feel him stiffen, feel his body shudder when I roll my heat over him. Dain growls, a predatory, otherworldly sound that sends fear coursing through my veins with the pleasure. He trails his lips down my neck, sucking and licking and biting at me like a man possessed.

I gasp, pleasure flooding through me as he laps at a bite mark he left on me. My hands clench around his shoulders, back arching. His lips move down the neckline of the dress and he nips at my collarbone. I open my eyes, lips parted as a silent keen escapes me. I wonder briefly if Dain will leave bitemarks over my entire body. He looks up at me and for an instant I coil away from him in fear. His eyes look completely black in the dim light; his lips twisted into a gruesome smile.

I blink, and the frightening image falls away; it's just Dain. But then his hands are roving my back, his hips moving against me. I gasp sharply as his nails prick my skin, but my eyes slip closed when his lips find mine again. No one has kissed me like this, with such ferocious need, in my entire life. I feel powerful, I feel strong. Even with Dain's hands guiding me roughly, and his lips making demands, I feel power coursing through me.

He pulls away just as I'm contemplating slipping out of this silk dress Altair bought me. Dain's hands hold me still, and I pant, eyes wide as I stare into his gaze. He smirks, not a hair out of place despite my hands raking through it. Gently, He lifts me from his lap and sets me onto the bench beside him. He picks up the book, which fell into the grass when I lost myself. Reverently, Dain dusts it off and presses it into my hands.

"Take good care of it, Verity," he purrs.

He rises, looming over me. My eyes dart over him, taking in his strong, lithe figure. I bite my lip, resisting the urge to beg him to stay a while longer. Stay forever. He smiles as if he can sense my thoughts. His hands cup my cheek in a silent farewell.

"Wait," I blurt, jumping to my feet. He stops, looking at me expectantly. "When can I see you again?"

His smile broadens, his eyes black. "Soon, my love."

"My love?" I echo as he melts away into the trees.

I sink back onto the bench, clutching the book to my chest. It thrums with power, but I don't feel the overwhelming curiosity to read it now. I want Dain. I want him back with me in the dark, handling my body like he owned me. I shudder, biting my lip as I revel in my memories of the kiss.

Slowly, I come back to myself. The candle has burned halfway, the wax melting over the metal frame of the bench. I turn to the last page I read and study the words. Dain is in the back of my mind, my body still pulsing with desire and pleasure. I need to see him again. I need to ask him more about the book. There's something different about him, something more. He radiates quiet power, stronger than Altair. He's addictive, I admit with a shudder.

The book draws me back as my eyes settle over the jagged lettering. My thoughts stray from Dain and my body cools as I read. I feel a shiver along my spine, as if someone is watching me. But I can't seem to care enough to glance up. I can't seem to care about much anymore.

CHAPTER 13

ALTAIR

Navi turns to me, her eyes cold and fierce. "What is going on, Altair? Did you see the way her eyes changed?" Navi purses her lips and tightens her grip on the hilt of her sword, pacing.

"I saw," I murmur. I lean against the heavy oak table with the remnants of my dinner with Verity.

"Something isn't right with her," Navi continues. She eyes me. "I take it there's been no progress with wedding preparations?"

"Not yet," I say, tapping a finger against my folded arm. I stare into the flames in the fireplace, wishing they held answers. "But she will."

"Are you sure?" Navi moves closer. Her concern is clear in her emerald green eyes. "I've served you for many years, Altair. I was by your side throughout the curse. If she doesn't fulfill her covenant to you, I'm afraid it will all be for nothing."

I purse my lips. "We don't know what happens if it isn't fulfilled. It could be nothing."

"And if it isn't?" Navi asks. "We can't afford to find out."

"I know," I sigh. "The more I pressure her, the more she pulls away."

"She's a woman," Navi says. "Show her your affection isn't completely due to the curse."

I shove away from the table, frustration sweeping through me. "Haven't I done that already?"

Navi rolls her eyes. "I wouldn't know, I'm not watching your relationship with her that closely."

The frustration falls away almost instantly as I watch Navi's eyes drop to her sword. "I'm sorry," I say softly. "I shouldn't burden you with this."

"No." She looks up. "This concerns us all."

I sigh, the burden of my duties settling like a heavyweight on my shoulders. "I know."

Navi moves beside me. She smiles, the same smile she gave me before Verity arrived. "Go to her, let the councilors take over for a few days. It will be worth it."

"Thank you, Navi," I whisper.

She puts a hand on my shoulder and squeezes. Navi drops my gaze as she releases me. With a short bow, she sweeps out of the room. I bite my lip, considering her last advice, and move to the window.

A war is coming. I won't relish the bloodshed we will face, but if we can finish the Bloodbane, Alnembra won't be disturbed for thousands of years to come. We will have peace. I grit my teeth as I picture Maaz in her stone keep, plotting against me. On the battlefield, I will find her and kill her myself. I will kill her for what she did to me, for what she has done to my people, and for what she did to Verity.

The wound on Verity's stomach is nothing but a thin scar now. I wonder absentmindedly if it bothers her. Navi is right, I haven't given Verity much of my time lately. I haven't even bothered to ask her how her recovery is going, I realize with a pang of guilt. I've hardly wondered how she spends her days, or if she's lonely. I slam my fist against the stone wall, cursing myself. I brought this on myself. I drove her away first and then expected her to wait for me.

It's late, but I doubt she'll be sleeping. I'll go to her now. I take one last long look out the window when movement in the darkness below catches my eyes. I lean against the window pane, peering into the shadow. It's Verity, picking her way through the gardens towards a secluded copse of trees in the back. I narrow my eyes, curiosity lancing through me. She disappears into the thickly wooded area. A second later, I see the faint glow of candlelight behind the foliage.

What is she doing? I frown thoughtfully, staring at the light penetrating the darkness. Suspicion pricks at me, sending a tingling sensation down my back. I wonder if this has anything to do with her interest in the Bloodbane, her incessant questions. There's movement against the trees and I see a Fae man slip into the shadows. I press myself against the glass, fingers digging into the cold surface as I stare. I recognized him; I've seen those narrow shoulders before. The gardener.

My heart is pounding, fury and suspicion flooding through me as I sprint out of the room. I rush down the stairs, ignoring the soldiers that start after me curiously. I wave them away as I take the grand staircase to the main floor. My footsteps echo back at me from all sides, a staccato beat as I run. All I can think of is Verity in the garden alone with a stranger. He could hurt her. He could woo her.

I leap from the stairs onto the gravel path leading to the back gardens. The gravel crunches beneath my hurried footsteps. The air is chilly outside despite the summer night. The copse of trees comes into view and I slow in case Verity is calling for help. But the night is silent; no night birds sing, no insects chirp. I move into the trees quietly, careful to step only on clear ground.

Verity comes into view and I duck behind a tree trunk. I study her from my hiding place. She's illuminated by the candlelight, sitting on an old, rusted bench. There's a book open in her lap.

And beside her, is the man I saw. His arm is draped around her, his eyes locked on her as she reads from the book. At times, his fingers stroke along her back and she shudders to awareness; as if she was lost and he drew her back again.

I clench my hands into fists at my side, unable to turn away. She stares at the same page for hours before finally moving on. Her eyes are hazy, a ghost of a smile on her lips as she reads. He must have done something to her, I realize, anger coiling around my heart. Verity left me to meet in secret with this man. They share something between them, something that has pulled Verity away from me.

I close my eyes, resisting the urge to burst into the clearing and tear apart the strange man. That would only push Verity away even more. But, oh, it would certainly satisfy me to have his blood coating my hands. Blood is roaring in my ears as I open my eyes again. The book falls to the wayside as Verity climbs smoothly into his lap. A small cry escapes my lips as they kiss. He's rough with her, cruel even. He pinches and bites, but she revels in it. Her soft moans reach my ears as she arches into him. Verity moves against him, writhing like she's possessed.

I feel a sharp pain in my chest as they lose themselves in each other. I had fallen in love with Verity. I wanted her to love me back. And yet, here she is. With another man. Sorrow overtakes me. I wish I could look away, but I can't. My gaze is locked on them, as if I'm punishing myself for having let her slip this far away.

Finally, the man pulls away. Verity's brows crumple as he leaves her. But soon, her eyes are roving over the pages of her book again. I watch the man melt into the shadows. Fury overcomes the heartbreak I felt only seconds before. I follow him, my blood pounding in my ears. I grind my teeth, hands clenched into fists at my side. I'll rip his limbs from his body first.

I find him on the garden path, meandering towards the walls. I fall into step behind him, waiting for him to notice me. He stops, his back towards me. His hands are stuffed into his pockets as if he doesn't have a care in the world. Slowly, he turns to face me. My eyes narrow as I take in his wide grin and his black eyes.

"Altair," he says jovially. "Verity isn't here. I'm afraid she's in the other direction."

"I know," I growl, hardly caring that he didn't bother to use my title.

His grin broadens, stretching so far it sends a prick of fear through me. "Oh, you saw that, did you? How did you find it? A valuable lesson perhaps? Your Verity can be quite wicked when she wants to."

I close the distance between us in a single lunge. I tackle him, driving him back against the wall. He chuckles as I thrust my forearm against his neck, crushing his windpipe. "How dare you?" I hiss.

"I didn't do anything she didn't want," he says, his eyes lit with mirth.

"Like hell you didn't." I growl.

The gardener barks out a laugh. "You hardly know her, Altair. You know her less than she knows herself."

"And you do?" I demand, thinking of all the ways I could kill him.

"Of course I do," he snaps. He calms, closing his eyes for an instant. "I know her better than she knows herself. That's why she seeks me out."

My heart feels as if it's been dowsed in icy water at his words. How many times have they met? I wonder, nausea welling through me. I want to believe that it has nothing to do with Verity, that it's simply a mistake she made while trying to find answers. But I feel a prick of doubt in the back of my mind as I glower at the stranger. What if there truly is something between them?

"Who the fuck are you?" I demand, growling.

"I'm the gardener." He grins. "I make things grow. Even poisonous things."

My narrowed eyes relax for an instant as I study his black gaze. His smile is gone, and the black of his pupils extends over his irises and into the white of his eyes. I steel myself against the fear that coils in my gut.

I snarl and choke him. He coughs, blinking back tears. "I want you out of my sight," I growl. "I want you out of the palace and to never return. Do you understand?"

"I understand," he chokes out, the wicked grin returning. "But Verity will be sad to see me go."

"She'll never think of you again," I say furiously.

He laughs, the sound powerful and chilling. "You may as well forget marrying her. She doesn't love you, and you could never satisfy her."

"And you think you could?" I ask, my voice harsh.

"She'll have another groom soon, of that I'm certain," he purrs.

A frozen wind blows against me as his eyes darken once more. I lurch away from him as fear clenches my heart. Something isn't right about this man. He's no gardener. He pushes away from the wall and straightens his tunic with a bright smile. He pushes past me, disappearing into the darkness and leaving me reeling. I don't consider myself an easily intimidated person. But something about his eyes had my breath locked in my throat from fear.

I stare into the shadows he melted into for what feels like hours, waiting for him to return with the wings of a demon or some other monstrous creature. But he's gone. I find my breath again and head back to the copse of trees. The candlelight is low, and somehow, dawn is on the horizon. I spent all night in the gardens, but it felt like mere hours.

Verity is draped on the mossy ground beside the bench, sleeping. Her cloak is tucked around her, her silk gown no doubt ruined from the dirt and damp of the ground. She sleeps soundly, her lips softly parted. She looks angelic almost. But I can't forget the way she moved against the stranger. I can't forget the way she responded to his body.

My eyes drift over the book beside her, propped open. I crouch and pick it up. The leather binding is warm, as if it was just barely in Verity's hands. I flip it open, eyes roving over the page. The writing is harsh and jagged, difficult to read. But the sketching in the margins are clear enough. It's a book on Bloodbane rituals and magic. The text is filled with spells and cruel rituals they use to practice their magic.

My gut coils and I feel nauseous as I read about the rituals they perform in the ether. No Fae has ever found a portal into the ether, the realm of the old gods, and it's strictly forbidden. But the Bloodbane draw most of their magic from the other realm. Sadal Melik waits for them in the ether. They give him blood and life force to sustain him through dark rituals. It's sickening.

I swallow the bile rising in my throat as I study the pictures and text. I flip through more pages, panic rising in my chest. This is what Verity has been reading? This is why she's so secretive? I bite the inside of my cheek. My father destroyed all the books in the kingdom about Bloodbane magic in an attempt to stop them from gaining anymore power. I don't know how Verity got her hands on this book, but I have no doubt it's related to the mysterious gardener.

Poisonous flowers indeed, I muse.

CHAPTER 14

VERITY

The green glow of the sun through leaves teases me from my sleep. I take a long breath, sighing. I can feel dew on my skin and along my cloak; cold little buttons of water. I stretch, breathing in the earthy scent of soil and moss. Dain is long gone by now with the sun already rising. My stomach turns as I remember what happened the night before. I don't know what came over me that I would let him handle me like that. I betrayed Altair.

Suddenly, as I roll over, I see glistening leather boots covered in dew. I gasp and lurch away, coiling into a crouch. It's Altair. He stands stiffly, as if he's been in the same place all night. His brows are pinched, his lips twisted into a deep frown. He doesn't look at me, his eyes are locked onto the book in his hands. My book.

My voice hitches in my throat as I see him with my precious, dangerous secret. I release a strangled noise and lift a hand towards him. His eyes dart away from the text to meet mine and I'm struck by the intensity of his hazel gaze. He snaps the book shut with a thud and narrows his eyes at me.

"So, this is what you've been hiding," he murmurs, turning it over in his hands. "This must be one of the last Bloodbane texts in existence. How did you get it?"

"I found it," I stammer even though the lie sends bile rising in my throat.

"You found it," he echoes, his voice soft. "Tell me, did the gardener have anything to do with it?"

My heart stops in my chest. "What gardener?"

Altair laughs mirthlessly, tossing his head back. "Verity, do you take me for a fool?" His laughter ends abruptly, and he glowers at me. "I saw you last night."

This is my worst nightmare. I swallow the nausea threatening to overwhelm me and struggle to my feet. Altair is staring at me coldly, as if I'm an insect on the bottom of his shoe. I wrap my cloak tighter around myself defensively. "I don't know what you're talking about. I came here to read. I knew the book was forbidden so I brought it here to read in secret."

"Little truths to cover a lie," he murmurs. "But I know what I saw. I was right there."

The blood in my veins runs cold as he points to a spot a yard away behind a thick trunk. He would have had a perfect view of my intimate act with Dain. I bite my lip. "I'm sorry," I whisper.

"You're sorry?" He hisses. "You are supposed to be my wife within the month. Yet you betrayed me."

"It's not as if either of us is in love with the other," I say, desperately searching for an excuse. "Our relationship is a facade."

"Our relationship," he repeats, trailing off. I can see the muscle in his jaw twitching as he grinds his teeth. "You aren't who I thought you were."

I feel a flash of anger at his words. "You never knew me at all." I narrow my eyes.

"I thought I did," he says, his voice losing its furious edge. He sighs. "I thought you were kind, funny, and beautiful. But all I see is a twisted, unhappy, lost girl."

Twisted? Lost? I bristle, straightening my shoulders. "You have no idea what it's like," I hiss. "No idea how it feels to suddenly discover you aren't who you thought you were – that you have an evil inside of you. I just want to know who I am."

Altair looks at me sadly. "I could have told you who you were a week ago."

His words send a lance of pain through my heart. "Altair," I whisper.

"I care about you, Verity," he says, closing the distance between us. I try to pull away, but he snatches my wrist. "I want you to be happy. I want us to be happy. Stop keeping such secrets from me."

My lips part in surprise at his confession. And then his mouth is on mine, kissing me desperately. I yelp in surprise, but the sound is muffled. I'm stiff in his arms as he holds me close to his chest. But I don't pull away. He's soft and gentle with me, the opposite of Dain's embrace. Slowly, I ease into him, relaxing. His tongue eases my lips further apart and our tongues tangle together. I feel a surge of passion as he deepens the kiss, nipping softly at my bottom lip.

Heat swarms through me like a fire blazing through a dry meadow. My nails dig into his back, pushing our bodies closer together. My head grows clear as we kiss and something in my chest clenches tightly. This is how I used to feel around Altair all the time. Our kisses, the few we had, were headier than this – more passionate and freer. He's careful with me now, as if I'm a fragile doll. His hands rove down my back to cup my ass, squeezing tightly. I gasp, arching into him.

Both hands. The book.

I wrench away from him, eyes wild. I stare at his empty hands as he looks at me with confusion. The book is gone. "The book," I pant, searching. "What did you do with the book?"

Altair is silent as I drop to my hands and knees and peer under the bench. I see it then, tucked half way beneath the root of a tree behind the bench. I drop to my stomach and grunt, straining for it. When I feel the warm leather binding in my hands again, I sigh. The tight sensation in my gut eases as the book is safe in my hands.

I look up and see Altair studying me pityingly. Shame washes through me as he turns on his heel and disappears into the foliage. Sometimes, we don't need words to hurt someone. I kneel on the wet moss, book in my lap, staring at the place he disappeared into. There's no chance at healing the chasm between us. Altair will have given up on me now. This is likely the last betrayal he will tolerate.

I feel something in my chest coil tightly, painfully. I shove the sensation aside and hold the book to my breast. All I want are answers. I want to know my history; why I have the Bloodbane oath running through my veins, waiting for Sadal to awaken it. Altair doesn't want me to find those answers. He wants me to be content as the mortal, Verity. But I have too many questions for that. And although I don't want to betray him, it seems more and more that I'm coming to cross-roads.

Altair, or myself?

I bite my lip, fighting the tears welling in my eyes. I used to think marrying Henry would be hard. Now I know that I'm beginning to learn the meaning of the word. My fingers tighten around the book until my knuckles are white.

CHAPTER 15

I pace at the top of the keep, the howls of the demonic army echoing through the mountains. I hiss in response, trying to drown out the noise. For days now, the creatures from the ether have hunted in our mountains, waiting for the order to march on Alnembra. The few animals that roamed the mountains have scattered or been eaten. I've warned the covens to stay out of reach of the vile creatures. After what happened to our youngest coven, I can't allow anymore of my sisters to fall prey to the demons, or to Sadal's sick machinations.

The creatures' roars grow louder as they chase one of their weaker members. I stare down at them, frozen in place. Black blood arcs through the air as the limbs are torn from the smaller demon. They fall upon the corpse, yellow teeth digging into its flesh. I watch, fascinated and disgusted at the same time as the corpse is devoured in seconds. The creatures disperse once the meat is gone. Soon, the howling resumes. I shudder back to my senses and feel a curl of anger as they sniff hungrily at the base of the keep.

Maaz has practically abandoned the Bloodbane to attend to Sadal. She spends much of her time with him or admiring the army he gave her. She has abandoned her duties to lead, which has forced me to take her place. Even now, she's roaming the ranks of the horde. I grind my teeth as I think of the responsibilities she's shirked. I rule in her stead, but not in name. No, Maaz would never deign to admit that she rules in name only now. The covens are ecstatic, eager to move on Alnembra. Little do they know once our armies are done with Alnembra, there will be nothing left for us. Our mountains are barren now, and soon Alnembra will follow.

I wanted Alnembra because it was my home before I joined the Bloodbane. But I know that if Maaz gets her way, there will be nothing left. What Sadal would want with an ashen landscape devoid of life, I can never imagine. What's the point of power if there's no one left to rule? I turn, looking towards the door that leads down into the keep, but it's closed tightly.

"It's an impressive sight, isn't it?" Sadal asks from behind me.

I pivot, eyes narrowed. He's standing against the stone railing of the keep, staring out over the horde. Sadal is dressed in black, as usual. His pale skin is perfect in the murky sunlight. He rakes a hand through his black hair. I curl my lip at him, not bothering to hide my disdain. "That isn't the word I would choose," I say coldly.

He cocks his head at me, a smile playing over his lips. "You continue to surprise me, Cleo. Your distaste for me is refreshing."

"My Lord." I bow my head in a show of apology.

"Don't," he snaps. "Don't lie to me."

I purse my lips, anger flashing through me at his sharp tone. "As you wish."

"Very good," he sighs. "Now, why did you call me here?"

I pull back, confused. "I didn't."

"Come now, I can sense your intentions. If not now, you would have." Sadal cocks his head at me, waiting. "Speak freely."

I hesitate. I have ideas; ideas that Maaz has disregarded. She insists that Sadal gave her this horde of demons because it's the only way to defeat Altair. But I suspect differently. I hadn't planned on speaking to Sadal without Maaz, but I know Maaz would never let me question her in front of Sadal. He sought me out, I tell myself.

"I have an alternative solution that may interest you." I finally say.

Sadal splays his hands. "Go on."

"If you take this horde through Alnembra, they will destroy everything. The villages, cities, field, and forests will be burned. The Fae murdered. You will rule nothing but ash and darkness. What if I could conquer Alnembra for you without bloodshed?" The words spill from my open lips as my excitement grows.

If I can save my sisters and the Fae, then perhaps we can live in peace without the tampering of the Fae in a land of bounty. We wouldn't have to scrape to survive in these mountains or steal from border farms.

"And how would you propose to do this?" Sadal asks, raising a brow. "I have my hooks in Verity already."

"I want to go further," I say fiercely. "I want to destroy Altair's kingdom from the inside out."

"Subtle." Sadal smiles.

I grin viciously. "Perhaps you won't need to conquer an entire kingdom if I give it to you."

"What do you mean?" He asks, his lips twisted into a strange smile.

"Wouldn't it be simpler if the ruler of Alnembra simply gave in to your wishes?" I ask, moving to his side.

"Altair would never surrender without a fight," Sadal says dismissively.

"I'm not talking about Altair. I'm talking about the mortal Bloodbane." I peer up at him. "What if the ruler of Alnembra was groomed by you?"

Sadal stares appraisingly at me before leaning back against the railing. A chill wind blows over the keep's tower, rustling my cloak. "What did you have in mind?"

"Moving in the shadows, in the dark, like the Bloodbane witches were always meant to do," I whisper fiercely.

"You always were the clever one," he murmurs, grinning at me. "It's why you're my favorite wife."

My stomach turns at his praise and I twist away from him. "Does this mean you'll send the horde back to the ether?"

"I'll consider it," Sadal says as he pushes away from the railing and strides towards the door. He glances over his shoulder and I study his handsome profile. "Show me what you can do first."

My heart beats wildly as he disappears into the keep. I rush to my deadwood broom and swing my leg over it. Excitement sweeps through me and I smile to myself. My hood conceals my grin, casting a long shadow over my face. I launch myself into the sky, soaring high over the writhing black mass of demons below. I imagine I see Maaz's red cloak below. I leer at her, realizing that if I am successful, Sadal's conquest will be due to my efforts alone. I will be the most powerful Bloodbane in history.

My grin broadens as I imagine usurping Maaz. I was content to work in the shadows and play her games. But when she gave in so quickly to Sadal's demands, I realized I couldn't anymore. It's time for a new age for the Bloodbane. An age of power and prosperity under new rule. If I work my spell properly, no Bloodbane will be harmed in Sadal's conquest of Alnembra. The demons will disappear, and with them, my guilt and shame about what I did to the young coven.

My stomach turns as I remember their terrified faces as the creatures ripped into them. Their screams have echoed through my mind for these last nights, like ghosts haunting my memory. I used to be fierce and willful like Maaz. I used to be the kind of witch that joined in the bloodletting because it made me feel powerful. But I learned slowly that the real power is in the shadows; it's in the background where rulers twitch our strings like marionettes. I let Maaz believe she was pulling my strings all these years, but now it's time. It's time to show her my true strength.

I grin as the Bloodwood comes into view. Thankfully, this haven in the mountains hasn't been torn through by the horde yet. I doubt Sadal or Maaz will stop them from settling in our most sacred place besides the Holy Rite. The two of them seem content to let every Bloodbane tradition and belief fall to the wayside in their quest for power.

The Bloodwood is a copse of trees on the mountaintop. The trunks and leaves of the trees have been stained red due to the iron in the water that seeps into their roots. The strange coloring was what first attracted the Bloodbane to the trees. I land lightly in the center of the grove of trees, besides a flat boulder that serves as an altar.

Swiftly, I lay out the makings of my spell and draw a stick of chalk from my cloak. Murmur under my breath as I draw out the sigils of my spell across the rock. I slip my blade from my belt and hold it over my open palm. Every Bloodbane spell should be accompanied by a blood sacrifice. Many Bloodbane use the blood of another, a Fae victim or animal. I prefer my own, I've always found it to be more potent. With a smooth gesture, I slice my palm open. Pain shoots through my hand, hot and pulsing as blood pours freely from the wound.

The curtain of blood drapes over the stone, sinking into the chalk etchings. I murmur softly to myself, repeating the dark and powerful phrases of my spell work. I pour my intentions into the spell as I let my blood drip over it. I pour my wishes and my vision into it. Wind rushes around me, powerful and fierce. It whispers to me and a chill trails down my spine.

Soon, Alnembra will be ours. It will be for the Bloodbane.

Our conquest will be our crowning achievement. No longer will we be pushed to the fringes of society for our dark worship. We will rule. Grinning, I clench my hand into a fist and squeeze. The blood pours thicker and my smile broadens.

CHAPTER 16

VERITY

I stand in the center of the hall, staring at the closed oak door leading to Altair's office. I twist my lips, biting down hard. After our last encounter, I'm not looking forward to this. But I need to speak with him.

I'm surprised that Navi isn't standing guard outside the door, but I'm grateful for her absence. I have no doubt that if Altair told her what I had done that she would cut me down where I stand. I close my eyes, imagine her broad sword swinging towards me. I fear I deserve it what for I've done to Altair. I betrayed him; I don't know if he even still wants me. But the two of us are linked now, there's no avoiding that.

I straighten my back and smooth the fabric of my pale blue gown. Chewing the inside of my cheek, I knock lightly. The door opens, and I see Navi glowering at me. Of course, I think wryly. Navi scowls buts steps aside to let me pass. I see her elegant hand wrapped around the hilt of her sword.

When she steps aside, I see a dark, glossy table surrounded by Fae. Altair sits at the head of the table, his councilors on either side dressed in fine robes of silk. I spot Thal in the ranks, but he doesn't smile at me. His eyes are shadowed, his brows furrowed. I drop his gaze, shame flitting through me. Slowly, my eyes return to Altair. He stares emotionlessly at me, as if bored. He leans back into his velvet chair, arms draped over the sides.

"Verity," he says, cocking a brow. "To what do we owe this pleasure?"

I swallow back the angry retort boiling inside me. He doesn't appear to be as disturbed my presence as I am by his. I know he's still furious at me. I can see it shining in his eyes despite how much he tries to hide it.

"Altair," I mutter.

"Your Grace," Navi snaps from behind him. "You will address him as Your Grace."

I turn, eyes narrowing. Navi and I stare each other down for a moment and I grind my teeth together. "Verity," Altair says, his voice ringing powerfully. "What can I do for you?"

What can he do for me? My heart clenches. I don't deserve much from Altair. His question might be hollow and lacking sincerity, but he would ask me despite what I've done. I turn back to him, trying to stand tall. "A week," I say stiffly.

He cocks a brow. "A week?"

"I want to be married within the week," I continue, clasping my hands tightly behind my back so he can't see how white my knuckles are.

Altair sits silently for a moment, his eyes locked on mine. "Get out," he says, lifting his chin. "We'll continue the meeting in a few moments."

I gape at him. He's kicking me out? But it's his councilors that stand. Their chairs scrape loudly against the stone floor, their robes rustling. I purse my lips as the Fae sweep around me without even meeting my gaze. Only Thal keeps his eyes locked on mine. The door closes gently behind them, leaving Altair and I alone.

He rises, his tunic unbuttoned enough to expose his chest and collarbones. He bends over the long table and lifts his eyes to mine. "Come closer, Verity," he says.

Reluctantly, I move to his side and study the map laid out in front of us. Altair points to the mountain range along the border of Alnembra. "The Bloodbane witches have made their home in these mountains for thousands of years. Imagine being exiled into a single location for the length of your immortal life. They must be desperate to expand," he murmurs.

"Well what's in the other direction? Why Alnembra?" I ask.

"It's a barren wasteland across the mountain," he explains. "Nothing but a salty desert."

"Then they have nowhere else to go," I say, stroking the map.

"So it seems," Altair mutters, his eyes narrowing. "What made you change your mind?"

"About what?" I ask, my eyes locked on the symbol of the Bloodbane keep.

Altair rolls the map up, covering the Bloodbane keep, and sets it aside. I turn to look up at him. He's leaning against the table, his arms crossed impatiently over his chest. "The wedding."

I press my lips together tightly. "Something is wrong with me, Altair."

His eyes soften and I know that no matter what I've done, he pities me. "What do you mean?"

"Ever since I broke the curse, I've felt something different inside me; something deep down." I twist away from him, blinking back the tears that threaten to spill from my eyes. "I don't understand who I am anymore, or what I want. Before I broke the curse, when I looked at you, it was like I was in a dream. Now I can't wait to wake up."

"Perhaps we awakened something within you when we broke the curse," Altair murmurs, his hand stroking my shoulder.

I pull away from him, wiping at my eyes. "It doesn't matter now. I want to be married by the end of the week, maybe then I'll feel like myself again."

He presses his lips into a thin line, his hazel eyes narrowed with concern. "That simply isn't enough time to prepare."

"I don't care if it's a big wedding or if hardly anyone is there. It could be just the two of us," I say desperately.

"Our wedding is meant to draw Alnembra back into the world and strengthen ties with our allies." Altair shakes his head.

I feel a flash of inexplicable anger. "Then we'd better get to work."

His eyes glimmer and he moves back to his seat. "Then it will be done."

I wrap my hand around the door knob and tug it open. "Thank you, Altair."

"Verity," he says. I pause and glance at him over my shoulder. "Stop reading the book. Burn it if you can."

I run my tongue over my lips, anxiety flooding me. "Why?"

"I don't think it warrants an explanation," Altair says bitterly. "The book is leading you down a dark path."

"It's just a book," I mutter.

"No," he says. "It's not."

I know he's right. I know the book is powerful enough to pull me away from myself and deeper into my Bloodbane past. But I don't know if I can deny the magnetic pull I feel from the text. I don't know if I can deny all that Dain has promised I'll find in the book. My hand trembles on the knob. I push through the door, stepping back into the hall without another word to Altair. I can feel his eyes on me until the door closes shut again.

The skirts of my gown swirl around my feet as I head to my room. The book is safely hidden behind the wardrobe. I draw it out after locking my door. The sun is shining brightly outside. I curl up on the balcony with the book on my lap to read in the sun. Altair's words echo through my mind as my eyes rove the pages. I shouldn't be reading this. I know that. I've known that since Dain first put the book in my hands in the library. But I don't want to stop reading it. I'm fascinated by its mysteries. And

I sense that if I stop reading it, Dain will be nothing but a distant memory.

I twist my lips into a frown as I think of Dain. I should never have betrayed Altair in that grove of trees, but I know in my heart that if given the chance, I would do it again. Dain need only say the word and I would run to him. I shudder, chills tingling up and down my spine at the realization. I grip the book so tightly my knuckles go white. I can only hope that my marriage to Altair will save me because I can't save myself.

My attention is drawn back to the book as my eyes catch the words Holy Rite. I stroke the ink, eyes scanning the page greedily. My stomach turns as I read of the unholy ritual the Bloodbane perform when a new female joins their order. The witches bring the initiate into the highest tower in their keep, a room with a portal that leads into the ether. I bite down hard on my bottom lip as I read of the ceremony that ties the initiate to Sadal. It turns my stomach, nausea sweeping through me. It's sickening and painful and no doubt pleasurable when Sadal claims the initiate for his own.

This is what I would have to endure to become a true Bloodbane; what I would need to do to complete the oath already running in my veins. Curiosity tugs at me, compelling me to read more. I bury my nose in the book, eyes roving over the illustration of the well that acts as a portal to the ether. In the drawing, blood drains down into the well as the initiate is stretched over it. Sadal is pictured there, his sharp nails digging into her flesh.

A cloud crosses the sun, shrouding me in darkness. It pulls me away from the book and I feel as if I surfaced out of the deepest depths of the ocean. I look up, lifting my gaze to the sky. And I see Altair gliding above me, the wind ruffling his dark feathers. He doesn't glance down towards me, instead heading off towards the harbor.

I glance down at the book. I gasp, seeing the sketch of the dark ritual. Its grotesque, blood spattered everywhere. I drop the book, fingers trembling as I look at the drawing with new eyes. I kick the book away with my foot and draw my knees up to my chest, shuddering. Altair's father was right to destroy the books about Bloodbane magic and rituals. It's dark and gruesome. I swallow the bile rising in my throat as my eyes drift over the book again.

I hear my door creak open. I lean around the wall and peer into my bedroom. Dain's smile catches my eye and I scramble to my feet. "Dain," I cry, running towards him.

His smile broadens, his eyes glittering. "Verity, darling, what's the matter?"

"The book," I stammer. "I can't read it any longer."

"Is that so?" He murmurs. He steps back, out of arms reach just as the door opens again.

My brows furrow as I take in the strange woman who slipped into my room. Her blonde hair is almost white, her skin an alabaster shade. Her pale blue eyes are cold despite the smile pulling at her lips. "Who are you?" I ask warily. My gaze darts towards Dain as my heart pounds. "Dain?"

The woman strides towards me, her petite frame swaying. I stumble backwards as she closes the distance between us. The last thing I see are her eyes, pale blue.

CHAPTER 17

ALTAIR

Flying cleared my head from my meeting with Verity. It seems every time I leave her, I'm left angry, confused at best. I take a seat in my council room, ready to continue with our business for the day. After Verity left, I postponed the meeting further to give myself some time to breathe. It shouldn't be this way. It shouldn't be such a struggle to be with the woman I love.

I drum my fingers on the heavy table. Love. I haven't told her how I feel, and if she pulls away further, I doubt there would even be a point. Someday my feelings will fade if there's nothing there to feed them. I'm pulled from my thoughts by Thal, who clears his throat pointedly.

"Altair?" He cocks a brow. "Are you ready?"

I sigh and straighten in my chair. "My apologies, my mind is preoccupied. Verity has made a decision on a wedding date." The councilors murmur happily at the news. I wait for them to fall silent. "She wants to be wed six days from now."

The councilors' eyes widen with surprise as they sit in shock. "That's impossible, we need more time to ensure our allies and trade partners can arrive comfortably," one of them blusters. "We must ask the Curse-Breaker to reconsider."

"Impossible," I say. "I've already tried. On this, she won't be swayed."

"Then we need to spread the news immediately," Thal says.

I nod. "I will go myself; I can cover the distances in a day."

The councilors mutter at my announcement, pursing their lips. They aren't pleased that I've kept the ability to change into my beastly form. They find any reminder of Maaz's power over us unpleasant. But if I have the power, I say why not use it.

Thal leans forward, clasping his hands together. "I'll go, I can be your emissary to at least a few of the kingdoms. Send out your fastest ships and ambassadors to the rest."

"You? Taking on a responsibility?" I cock a brow teasingly and grin.

He shrugs, chuckling. "What can I say? You've inspired me."

I press my lips together, considering his proposal. "You would likely only make it to Canes and Mensa, perhaps Stellium."

Canes and Mensa are important trade partners, our politics are different, but they are peaceful neighbors. It's vital that their ruling family can enjoy the wedding. Stellium is our greatest ally and has been since my father's rule. An island kingdom, they're lands are filled with sands and tropical trees. They rely on trade and a fair relationship with us for the rest of their goods. In return, we get exotic spices and a powerful naval ally. Stellium's ruler, Queen Haru, must be at the wedding.

"I will make it to all three," Thal assures me. "Lend me the Wind-Singer."

I bark out a laugh. The Wind-Singer was my father's personal sailing vessel. It hasn't seen the open ocean since his death, though I've kept it in good condition. "You want my father's ship?" I chuckle.

Thal looks at me seriously, and I know he isn't joking. "It's the fastest ship in Alnembra."

I purse my lips thoughtfully. "If you wreck it, if there's even a small scratch on the hull, I'll cut off your most prized possession, Thal."

"I spent almost a century at sea." Thal grins. "I'll be gentle."

I shake my head, a smile pulling at my lips. "Go now." I wave my hand to the door. "Bring a scribe with you, have them draw up invitations on the journey."

"As you will," Thal says, rising. He flashes me a grin from the door and bows his head sharply.

I trust Thal more than any of my councilors combined. My cousin was spoiled rotten for most of his childhood and adolescence. In the end, as the youngest of his brothers, he had no claim to a position of leadership. So, he carried on his carefree ways and eventually no one expected anything of him at all. But I've always known how loyal he can be to someone he thinks deserves it. I trust him to get my allies here in time for my wedding.

"This meeting is adjourned," I say to my councilors. "I need to meet with the scribes and ambassadors."

Without waiting for my councilors to disband, I stride from the room. I climb the staircases to the south tower where the scribes do their work near the messenger doves. I take the stairs two at a time, my heart pounding with excitement. Finally, Verity and I will be wed. Finally, the curse will be permanently removed. The marriage might even save Verity from herself and the Bloodbane clutches.

I push open the warped wooden door at the top of the stairs and step into a brightly lit room. It's scantily decorated, every surface covered in books, papers, quills, and ink. A lone scribe sits in the middle of the room, the scratching of his quill on paper filling the silence. I approach. He doesn't look up. A smile tugs at my lips as I wait, hands clasped behind my back. The scribes never paused in their work to honor my father either, it's just their nature. Their loyalty is to pen and paper, not men.

Finally, the scribe gently places his quill on the desk. He turns to me, his wizened face lined with wrinkles. "Your Grace," he murmurs, dipping his chin.

"I need invitations to my wedding drawn up immediately," I say, taking a seat across from him.

"Certainly, how many?" He dips his quill into his bottle of ink.

"Twenty, for now," I say. "How soon can you be finished?"

The scribe methodically and slowly jots down notes on his paper. "The end of the day, I'm sure."

I shake my head. "I'm sorry, I need them sooner than that."

"What is the rush?" He asks, raising his brows.

"The wedding is in six days." I grimace.

"Six days?" His furry brows shoot up even higher in surprise. "Your Grace, the time –"

"I know," I say forcefully. "Have them finished as soon as you can, make it a priority. When you're finished, find me."

I rise as he dips his chin in acknowledgement. I leave the old scribe to his work then. As the door closes, I hear the soft scratching of his pen against paper, moving quickly this time. I hurry down the stairs towards my ambassadors quarters to give them their instructions. They haven't been sent to the neighboring kingdoms yet, I was waiting until I felt that Alnembra was prepared to open relations again. But now there's no time to waste.

Suddenly, as I'm striding through the halls, I'm wrenched backwards. I whirl, snarling, but find Navi panting, her eyes wide. "Navi," I say, anger disappearing at the sight of her. Worry swirls in my chest, I haven't seen Navi look so fearful since the curse took hold. "What is it?"

"An army," she pants. "Our scouts have spotted a Bloodbane army only a week's march away."

My blood runs cold. "An army?"

"Demons." Navi shudders. "They said they looked like demons."

Fury and fear lance through me. I have no doubt that Maaz somehow got her hands on creatures from the ether, perhaps through some sacrifice and ritual to Sadal Melik. "How many?" I ask through gritted teeth.

"At least fifty thousand," Navi says, her voice soft.

"Fifty thousand?" I echo, my eyes wide.

"A host like that would decimate our armies," Navi murmurs.

I narrow my eyes at the stone floor. "Shit."

"Altair," Navi says, drawing my gaze towards her. "They're on the move."

"Get our armies together immediately. I want all of our men stationed along the border and I want our scouts watching the enemy very carefully. If they so much as piss, I want to know about it," I snap.

She bows sharply and jogs down the halls. I watch her disappear around the corner towards the barracks and rake a hand through my hair. I lean against a nearby wall, my gut coiling with fear. I had known that Maaz wouldn't leave me and my people alone, but I didn't expect her to find a formidable force so quickly. Alnembra's army is only starting to recover from the thousand-year curse. Our forces are low, and many of them lack training.

I bite down hard on my lip and push away from the wall. With war on the horizon, a wedding may not be possible. If the demon horde marches into our borders within the week, there simply won't be time for it. And I won't invite my allies to Alnembra on the brink of devastation.

There's an open window nearby and I climb onto the lip of it, staring down at the gardens three stories below. Without hesitating, I throw myself off of it. In mid-air I let Maaz's magic flow through me and change me into my beastly form. I spread my wings wide and catch the wind just before I hit the stones below. Quickly, I soar towards Desmarais' bay, where the Wind-Singer will still be anchored.

My shadow passes over Desmarais below, and my people glance upwards as I pass. I beat my powerful wings as the mast of the Wind-Singer comes into view. The deck is a flurry of activity, with Thal at the helm shouting orders. He looks up as my shadow darkens the deck, but he doesn't pause his preparations. I land deftly, the ship rocking slightly under my sudden weight.

"Altair," he says, tightening the moorings as I pad towards him.

"There's an army of demons from the ether on the move towards our borders," I say softly, not bothering to shift into my Fae form.

Thal pauses, his eyes widening slightly before he gets back to work. "What do you plan to do?"

"I want you to go to Mensa and Stellium, bring them the invitations. Don't mention the threat of war, but I want them here in three days if possible," I explain.

"And Canes?" Thal asks.

"I will go to Canes myself," I say, looking east. "He has the largest land army on the continent. I'll need it."

Thal shakes his head. "If he accepts."

I growl low, feathers ruffling. "He will accept."

"Good luck, cousin." Thal meets my gaze, pausing in his work.

I dip my chin towards him. "Same to you."

Thal turns to his men. "Get your asses moving!" He shouts, shoving a sailor aside to take over.

I launch myself from the deck, rustling the white sails of the ship. I head east, towards Canes. The Wind-Singer falls behind as I fly, and soon Desmarais is gone as well. I soar over open fields and forests, apprehension nestling in my gut. The great city of Civisilva is on the horizon as the sun reaches its apex in the sky. Civisilva is the last city in Alnembra before the border we share with Canes. The second largest city in Alnembra, it was built on an ancient ruin from a long-lost civilization. The forest has still reclaimed it, and its people live in harmony with the trees jutting through their homes and buildings, vines climbing all over the walls.

Verity would love Civisilva. My heart pangs at the thought of her. I want my Verity to return to me. I want to travel the world with her, to show her the vast and distant lands of this realm; places that used to be only fantasy to her. I fly low over Civisilva, peering down at the crumbling roads and roofs. When I return, I'll tell her of this place. Perhaps that will draw her away from the Bloodbane, if she had something else to occupy her.

Civisilva disappears into the forest as I cross the border into Canes. King Moritz has made his seat in the city of Suden, on Canes small coastline. It takes me less than an hour to make it to the city, and the sun hasn't yet begun to set. Suden is built on an incline, the highest point of which is Mortiz's castle. I only hope Moritz doesn't take it as a huge offense that I've arrived alone and unannounced.

I drop down outside the castle gates, amid a chorus of shouting. The people shriek, darting into alleys and down the road at the sight of me. Soldiers run along the ramparts; crossbows aimed towards me. I shift back into my Fae form and raise my arms to show that I have no weapons.

"I'm King Altair of Alnembra, here to see His Grace, King Moritz," I announce, shouting so my voice will carry to the soldiers.

A guard in the red armor of Canes's armies' jogs towards me. He studies my face and then shoves his sword against my back. I wince as the sharp point of the blade pierces through the leather tunic I wear. He urges me forward through the gates. I drop my arms and eye the soldiers as I pass. They stare emotionlessly at me, a well-trained unit intent on protecting their king.

Inside the walls, the grounds of the castle are nothing but stone. No trees line the walls, no grass grows. The castle is made of gray stone, drab with small windows. I haven't met with

Moritz for a thousand years, since before Maaz cursed me. Our last meeting wasn't promising.

I'm led through the grand doors and into a great throne room. It's three times the size of my throne room, with ceilings so high they disappear into shadows above me. Huge columns line the room, holding up the grand ceiling. My footsteps echo loudly as I approach the dais where Moritz is waiting on his throne. The dais is a full head higher than me, I crane my neck to look up. Moritz gazes imperiously at me, wrapped in a heavy red cloak despite the heat of summer.

His golden hair glimmers in the light of the torches that line the walls. His sharp eyes match perfectly with his sharp jaw and slim nose. Delicate and yet covered in hard edges, Moritz looks even more imposing than he did the last time we met. A thousand years my senior, he's ruled since I was a baby.

He stares down at me, colorless eyes glimmering. "You arrive unannounced outside my castle; in the beastly form you wore for the last thousand years. What is the meaning of this?" His powerful voice is at odds with his slim frame.

I dip my head in a shallow bow. "My apologies, King Moritz. But I have urgent business with you and little time."

"Come," Moritz says, rising. He strides down from the dais to stand before me. He purses his thin lips and waves away his soldiers. "Follow me."

Moritz leads me out of the throne room, towards a small door hidden behind one of the huge columns. He slams through it, not bothering to hold the door for me before it slams closed. Biting back an insult, I push through, following him towards the desk that sits in the center of the small room. I look around, taking in the book cases that line the walls and the various maps pinned to boards throughout. There are no windows, the only light coming from the chandelier above the desk and the blazing fireplace.

I tug at my collar, loosening it as heat washes over me. Moritz looks comfortable in the heat. He drapes his cloak over the chair behind the desk and sits down stiffly. I wait until he offers me a seat before following suit. I can feel sweat beading on my brow as the fire blazes.

Moritz eyes me. "I haven't seen you since before the curse. I heard you managed to find a mortal woman to break it. A Bloodbane woman."

"She's not a Bloodbane," I say bitingly, lounging back in the chair.

He shrugs. "Enough pleasantries." I resist the urge to roll my eyes. I can't imagine what he considers uncomfortable if he insists that our abrupt conversation was pleasant. "Why have you come?"

"I came to personally invite you to my wedding," I explain. "Verity and I will be wed in six days."

"Short notice," Moritz quips.

"My apologies," I say, dipping my chin again.

"I'm disappointed in you." Moritz shakes his head. "You seemed promising before Maaz cursed you. Now, I'm not so sure. But so far, I'm less than impressed."

I bristle. "Circumstances outside my control have forced my hand."

"You are a king," Moritz says bluntly. "There are no forces outside your control."

I inhale sharply at his brusque words. There isn't time to argue the finer points of duty. "There is a second reason for my visit today," I say. "A Bloodbane force of fifty thousand is marching on Alnembra."

"And yet you are planning a wedding?" Moritz's eyes glitter.

I purse my lips. "It's necessary. The curse, you understand." I don't wait for Moritz to reply before pushing on. "My army can't protect my people from the enemy forces. We need more men."

"My men, I presume," Moritz says. He leans back in his chair, looking thoughtful.

"Maaz won't stop at Alnembra's borders – you know that," I

say fiercely. "We need to stop them where they stand, before they grow more powerful."

"You may find that allies are in short supply," Moritz says. I narrow my eyes. "Rumors are swirling that your mortal woman has an unhealthy interest in the Bloodbane."

I purse my lips, fury lancing through me. There aren't many in the castle that know of Verity's recent change in behavior. But I won't tolerate a spy in the midst, or a gossip. "I don't know what you mean," I say stiffly. "Verity comes from the mortal realm; she knows nothing of magic and witches and Fae. She's simply curios."

"You know what they say about curiosity," Moritz murmurs.

"Yes," I say softly, my eyes flashing angrily. "I know what they say."

CHAPTER 18

Cleo

This mortal body is strange, I think as I study her pale, thin arms. Sadal is gone, having ensured that the spell went smoothly, he disappeared soon after. I almost felt sorry for the mortal when I saw her staring at Sadal, hoping he had answers for her. I clench my hand into a fist and then stretch out my fingers, testing this new body. It's weak, and I don't sense much magic in it either. I scowl, it will be difficult to cast spells in her body while maintaining my own enchantment. I'll have to be careful.

I stride through her room, towards the balcony where the precious Bloodbane text was abandoned. My reflection in the mirror catches my eye and I pause to study myself. To study her. Verity's eyes are the same pale blue that Maaz and I share. Her hair is a dusty brown shade and pulled into a loose braid. Her ivory skin is pale, a sickly pale with little color in her cheeks. I wonder if her coloring was always this way, or if it has something to do with her relationship with Sadal.

I pity her for falling so easily to his guiling ways. But Sadal has that effect on most people he meets. He had that effect on me once. Verity's eyes grow dark as I think of my early years with the Bloodbane. So many nights spent waiting for Sadal, craving him. I grew out of my fascination for him quickly in comparison to most. For that I'm grateful.

I take one last glance at this new body in the mirror before moving to the balcony. I collect the text and tuck it away in a secret place. When I accomplish my goals here, I will take the text back with me to the keep. Under Maaz's rule, we've lost many records and created even less.

I glance out the window and see a shadow streaking across the orange-hued sky. The sun is setting, and I spot the beastly form Maaz cursed Altair to wear in the sky. I smile as he draws closer, admiring his magnificent wings. It wasn't much of a curse, in my opinion. She made him stronger, fiercer, and angrier. She made an enemy.

I turn away from the balcony as Altair disappears over the castle turrets. I smile to myself; I'm looking forward to this next bit. I hope that Sadal is keeping his demonic horde from the march long enough for me to make my move against Altair. My plan is a delicate one, but in the end, it will be much more successful. If Maaz had any brains at all, she would have thought of this years ago. I sigh, shaking my head. If I had any guts at all, I would have suggested it long ago and saved the Bloodbane from hundreds of years of suffering.

The door opens, and a willowy Fae woman slips through the door. Her bright, emerald eyes rake over me with disdain and I smile, recognizing her gaze. She furrows her brows, mouth twisted into a frown. I'm not surprised that the Fae woman detests the mortal so much, now it all makes sense. The woman's hand wraps around the hilt of her sword as she closes the door behind her. I look at her expectantly, eyes narrowed.

"Altair has returned, he wants to see you," the Fae woman says stiffly.

I toss my braid over my shoulder and cross my arms. "Where is he?"

"In his rooms," she says. I don't miss the way her shoulders straighten and her jaw clenches.

I flash her a smile, baring my teeth at her. "It's good to see you again."

Her eyes narrow. "What?"

"It's been a while since we last spoke," I say. "I thought you might even keep in touch. After all, we made a great team."

Her lips press tightly together as her eyes widen imperceptibly. "You."

"Me." I grin. "All the information you fed to us when the mortal was brought into your realm was ever so helpful. Too bad it didn't work out for either of us."

"What are you doing here?" She hisses, drawing her sword. "Where is Verity?"

"As if you care," I scoff. I turn away, swaying towards the balcony. "I'm here on business. Business that could have once benefited you." I eye her over my narrow shoulders. "Now, I'm going to take away the one thing you love."

With a sharp war cry, the woman launches herself towards me. Her blade is poised above her, ready to swing down and rend my head from my shoulders. I fling my hand towards her, picturing my intentions. The woman's body flies towards the wall, crashing loudly into a bookshelf. Her head strikes the lip of one of the shelves, blood spurting from her skull. She sags to the ground, arms draped over the mountains of fallen books. Her sword clatters to the ground beside her and I kick it away under the four-poster bed with a grin.

Exhaustion tugs at my bones and muscles. The exertion of so much magic in this weak body is too much. Another spell like that, and I could lose control of Verity's physical form. Then I would have nothing. I pause, leaning against the bed to catch my breath for a moment. But I don't have any time to waste. If Altair is kept waiting long, he might seek me out himself.

I open the wardrobe and draw out a thin, black satin gown. I slip into it quickly, smoothing down my hair and checking my appearance in the mirror. The gown hugs Verity's curves and has a deep neckline that almost reaches her navel. I smile sinisterly at myself, running my hands over the fabric. It's the perfect gown for what I have in mind. But the necklace around Verity's neck isn't suitable for my needs. Carefully, I pluck it from my neck and lay it over the dresser.

I lock the room behind me and toss the key into a plant in the corner. My skirts rustle around my ankles as I sweep through the halls towards Altair's rooms. I knock lightly on the door.

"Come in," I hear Altair call.

I slip through the door, closing it softly behind me. Altair is standing at the balcony, staring out over Desmarais. I sidle up beside me. He hardly glances at me, instead taking a sip of wine from a goblet. I look out over the glowing city, like stars in the night sky.

"We've begun preparations for the wedding," he says, his voice stiff and subdued.

I glance curiously at him, waiting for him to elaborate. "Excellent," I say.

He's silent for a moment, eyes roving over the city. "Things will be different soon Verity. You need to be prepared."

Different? I furrow my brows. "What do you mean?"

Altair looks at me for the first time and I see the shadows behind his eyes. "I flew to Canes today to meet with an old friend," he says.

"I didn't know you had any friends," I tease, smiling.

He eyes me, tilting his head curiously. "I met with King Moritz because everyone in Alnembra, including you and I, will die by the end of the week without his help."

I widen my eyes, feigning fear. "What are you saying?"

"The Bloodbane have summoned a horde of fifty thousand demons. They're marching towards us as we speak." He takes a long drink, draining his goblet.

I narrow my eyes. The horde isn't supposed to move until Sadal knows I've failed. I shove aside my suspicions so I can continue to lead Altair on and fill Verity's shoes. "Will we be able to beat them?"

"Perhaps," he murmurs. "My old friend offered us an army on one condition." Altair purses his lips. "You must abandon completely your studies into the Bloodbane. You have to swear it. The Fae in Alnembra and throughout the continent are worried by your interest. I'm worried."

I feign innocence and surprise, widening my eyes. "Of course," I say. "Anything for you."

Altair looks at me curiously. "I've ordered dinner, care to stay?"

"I was hoping you would ask." I give him a simpering smile and thrust out my breasts, drawing his eyes. "I know things between us have been strange, and I'm sorry."

"Sorry?" He cocks a brow. "I'm not sure you know the word. Every time you apologize you toss it back in my face with new anger."

I keep my face a mask. It seems that Verity and Altair have been on bad terms, a fact that hopefully I can work to my advantage. "I'm a slow learner," I say, wrinkling my brows pitifully.

There's a knock at the door and a servant rolls a cart into the room. I wait in silence as the servant lays out dinner on the table and bows out. I let Altair hold my chair out for me before sitting, casually grazing his thigh with my fingers. His eyes drift over me as he takes a seat across from me.

"So, Canes," I say, fishing for information as we eat. "You've never spoken of Moritz before." I arch my brow, hoping I'm right.

Altair pours me a glass of wine. "No, we're not exactly the definition of friends. But Canes has always been good to Alnembra, and vice versa. I knew I could count on him, he's a thoughtful man."

"That's good news," I say, storing this information away for later. If I fail here, I will at least have information that might be vital to this war. Though I know I can't fail here.

I try to coax him into conversation, but Altair is subdued. I purse my lips. Since Maaz became obsessed with Altair and Alnembra, all I heard for hundreds of years was of his insolence and his similarities to Sadal. But all I see here is a man with the weight of the world on his shoulders.

I sigh and push my plate away. Altair looks up, chewing slowly as he eyes me. "Is something wrong?"

I look away. "I came here to reconcile with you, but it seems you're not in the mood."

"Reconcile?" He cocks a brow. "It was my impression that you apologized, and I accepted. Reconciliation accomplished."

"I meant to reconcile in other ways." I trail my fingers over my collarbone and down the slice of skin to my navel.

His eyes follow the soft movements of my hand and I see a flash of desire in his eyes. I rise, swaying around the table towards him. He watches me silently, and I wonder if I wore my Fae ears if I could hear the pounding of his heart. Smoothly, I drape myself over his lap, running a hand along his strong jawline. Altair inhales sharply and he grips my ass, holding me close.

"Forgive me," I whisper, leaning towards his lips. "For all of it."

Wordlessly, his lips close around mine in a passionate kiss. I lean into him, my breath stolen away. Desire flares in my body, a sensation that I haven't felt for many centuries. I curl into him, hardly caring that I'm pretending to be the mortal. I don't care how she kisses him or how she touches him, I want him for myself. I rake my fingers through his hair, pressing his face closer to mine as he deepens the kiss.

His tongue darts into my mouth and I hiss excitedly. I bite on his bottom lip, tugging on it as we kiss. His hand slips up my stomach towards my breast, easing over it. When he touches me, this body shivers with pleasure. I writhe against him, clinging to him as my body begins to truly crave him. Heat pulses through me like lava over a mountainside.

His hand trails from my breast towards my throat, stroking my skin gently. "Where is your necklace, Verity?" He asks with his lips pressed against mine.

I nip at him playfully. "I'll wear it for you later."

Suddenly, his hand tightens around my throat and I feel a thrill of fear in my chest. "Who are you?" He hisses.

"Altair, what are you doing?" I rasp, eyes wide with feigned innocence.

He laughs mirthlessly and stands, still holding me tightly. He drags me to the bed as I claw at his hand around my throat. With an icy glare, he tosses me onto the bed. Before I can squirm away from him, his hands are on my throat again, pinning me in place.

"Where is Verity?" He asks, his voice dangerously low.

"I'm right here," I exclaim, tears springing to my eyes.

Altair smirks at me, seeing right through my lies. I stare desperately up at him, trying to pry his fingers away from my throat. I can't fight him with my magic, I only have enough strength for one powerful spell before I lose control of Verity's body. I need her if I'm going to save my people by taking control of Alnembra using her influence over Altair. *Just until they marry,* I told Sadal. *Let me kill him myself and take the throne. I'll give you everything you want.*

But now, Altair has seen through my charade. And all because of one necklace.

"Tell me," he growls, "Where she is."

CHAPTER 19

Altair

My fingers tighten around Verity's throat. She chokes, her eyes bulging. I feel a hint of shame and fear as I squeeze. What if I'm wrong? What if this truly is Verity – just another one of her faces? But then she begins to laugh, an unpleasant, gurgling sound. She gives me a lopsided grin, baring her teeth at me.

"If you liked it rough, all you had to do was ask," she says teasingly. "What should our safe word be?"

I snarl, thinking back to the night I saw Verity with the stranger. Anger courses through me. "Shut up," I snap. "What have you done to her?"

"To who?" Verity asks innocently. "I'm right here."

I squeeze tighter, fearing that I'll leave bruises around Verity's pretty neck. I can't hurt her, not if this is truly Verity's body. I lean over her, eyes flashing. "End this charade now and I won't hurt you further."

"You won't hurt me at all," she whispers. "It's me. It's my body. You love me too much."

"Love you?" My brows twitch together. "Perhaps once I loved Verity, but I don't know you."

"That hurts," she pouts.

Suddenly, the door slams open and Navi stumbles through. Her sword is drawn and brandished towards me. Dried blood coats her face and mats her hair. She turns wild eyes on me. "Get away from her, Altair," she shouts. "That's not Verity."

"I'm aware of that, Navi," I growl.

She draws closer, her sword pointed at Verity on the bed. Verity blows her a kiss with a wink. "It's a Bloodbane witch," Navi says quietly at my side. "We should kill her."

Navi raises her blade over Verity, and Verity releases a throaty laugh. "Yes, kill me, Navi," she croons.

"Don't!" I shout, just as Navi starts driving down her blade. She pauses, the sharp edge only an inch from Verity's grinning face. "If you do this, you'll kill Verity."

"You don't know that," Navi growls.

"We can't risk it," I say through gritted teeth. "Stand back."

Suddenly, Verity squirms out of my grip, her leg slamming upwards into my groin. I double over, breath knocked out of me as burning pain overtakes me. Verity cackles and dances away from the bed towards the balcony.

"Altair!" Navi is at my side, crouching.

I wave her away. "Stop her," I cough.

Navi rises, swinging her sword to the side. "Gladly." She grins.

"Don't kill her," I pant, regaining my breath.

Navi gives me a curt nod before swinging at Verity. Fear floods through me as I watch Verity barely dodge Navi's blade. An image of Verity covered in blood, a dagger in her belly scrolls through my mind and I feel the same panic and anguish I felt only a month ago when Verity took Maaz's dagger for me. I rise to my feet and slip into a combat stance.

Verity dances away from Navi, a look of fierce determination on her face. I wonder briefly who we're dealing with, certainly not Maaz. I lunge towards her as she moves within reach. Her pale blue eyes dart towards me and then suddenly I'm flying backwards through the air. Black clouds my vision as I hit the stone wall with a dull thud. I groan, sinking to the floor. Through blurred and spotted vision, I see Navi turn anxiously towards me. Verity is on her then, clawing at her face. I reach towards them, trying and failing to get to my feet.

Navi's shouts and Verity's snarling echo in my ears as I lift a hand to my bleeding head. I've cut the back of my scalp, blood matting my hair. I wince as my fingers graze the wound. Navi cries out and tosses Verity onto her back, slamming her thin frame into the stone floor.

"No!" I yell, crawling towards them.

Navi glances at me, concern flashing in her eyes as she raises a fist above Verity's head. Verity's leg whips out, connecting with Navi's head with a crack. Verity jumps to her feet, snarling as Navi tries to regain her footing after the blow. I crawl to my feet, blinking back the blurry vision. Verity is panting heavily, a sheen of sweat on her brow. She's tiring, I realize.

I take advantage of it and dart towards her. She whips towards me and catches my fist mid-air. With an arrogant quirk of her lips she tosses me aside with supernatural force. Grimacing, I launch myself towards her and slam my fist into her side before she can dart away. She groans and doubles over. Regret lances through me as I see her face twisted in pain. Verity stumbles backwards, away from Navi who is rising to her feet with renewed bloodlust.

She chuckles at the sight of us closing in on her from two sides, backing her into a wall. "You must think you'll win this little game," she laughs, panting.

"It looks like I might." I cock my head at her. "Surrender now, give me Verity, and I won't hurt you."

"You think I care about pain?" She tosses her head back, releasing a joyless laugh. Her head snaps towards me again and she bites viciously. "Being a Bloodbane is pain. We embrace pain, we love it, we feed off it. Give me pain and you'll only see pleasure."

I twist my lips into a scowl. "I doubt that, Bloodbane."

Her eyes narrow, her teeth bared towards me. "There are different types of pain. It's most pleasant when I can hurt others. You understand."

"I understand," I murmur, "That you are a sick, evil woman. Release Verity."

"Do you remember the spy?" She asks. "Do you remember sending Navi, you're most trusted soldier, to find the spy that was selling out you and your people to Maaz?"

"What of it?" I mutter, glowering at her.

She smiles broadly and tilts her chin towards Navi. "She was in front of you the entire time."

My gaze slips towards Navi, her face is pale, eyes wide. Nausea sweeps through me and my gut twists. "Is this true?"

"Altair," Navi stammers.

Verity cackles, cutting her off. "I told you, Navi, we made a good team for a little while. But you're playing for the wrong side."

I stride towards Verity with renewed anger, my eyes flashing dangerously. She turns towards me, hand raised. With a shout, she tosses a frigid wind towards me. I dart to the side just in time to avoid the deadly strike of powerful air. Her eyes are wide with panic as I close the distance between us. I wrap my hands around her shoulders painfully as she begins to tremble violently.

Shaking, she tries to wrench free of my grasp. Verity gasps, her face twisted into a pained grimace. And then she collapses into my arms like a deadweight. I catch her, staggering, and lay her gently on the ground. Her eyes are closed, mouth open as she breathes softly. I brush Verity's pale brown hair away from her face, stroking her cheek gently. I can see the bruises forming from our short battle and my choking earlier.

From the corner of my eye, I see a woman scramble away.

Navi cuts her off, her sword ringing. I rise and stride towards the Bloodbane. Her red cloak hangs loosely around her shoulders and she stares defiantly at me with Verity's pale blue eyes. Her light golden hair shimmers in the candlelight – she's almost the spitting image of Maaz. But her eyes are sharper, more defiant.

She scowls at me, lips twisted viciously. "Kill me then," she hisses.

"I don't think so," I murmur. "Who are you?"

Her eyes widen, straying towards the balcony behind me. A chill wind howls through the air, and fear trickles down my spine. I turn as Navi's grip tightens on the Bloodbane. The gardener stands at the balcony door, a frightening smile stretching across his handsome face. Maaz's red cloak catches my eye and I swallow thickly. This is no ordinary gardener, and never was.

Maaz sweeps around the stranger and perches on the edge of my bed. "What a mess," she coos. "You really should hire new help, Altair."

"Maaz," I snarl. "You've brought a guest."

Maaz sighs contentedly, her blue eyes raking over the stranger's chest. "I brought my Lord, the Dark One."

My blood runs cols in my veins, like ice. My jaw twitches as I take in the gardener. But he isn't a gardener. He's Sadal Melik. My gut twists as I realize that Sadal Melik was in my home, seducing Verity under my nose. I was so worried about the threat of war, I didn't notice the battle taking place inside my own house. The battle for Verity's loyalty. I may have lost it already to the Dark God.

Sadal strides forward, still grinning. "It's been such a pleasure being hosted by you," he says smoothly.

I narrow my eyes at him, my gaze darting between him and Verity. "I can assure you the pleasure was all yours," I say through gritted teeth.

Sadal's eyes glimmer. "No need to fear. I'll take excellent care of her."

I lunge in front of Verity, blocking his view of her. "You will not," I snarl.

"Won't I?" He cocks a brow.

Maaz giggles and moves to the balcony, her cloak flapping in the wind. "This was always your problem, Altair – why you could never win against us," she says lightly, meeting my furious gaze. "You always stood up when you should sit down. You surrendered when you should have fought."

"Stay away from her," I growl as Sadal strides towards me.

He shoves me aside, launching me across the room with an icy touch. Pain shoots through my shoulders and ribs as I collide with the wall. Navi stands frozen beside the captured Bloodbane as Sadal slings Verity's unconscious frame over his shoulders. He grins at me, gloating. Growling, I throw myself at him, arms outstretched, wishing I had a dagger.

Laughing, he lashes out with his foot, kicking me in the chest. I hear a sharp crack and know that my ribs have been broken by the blow. I collapse with a cry as Maaz and Sadal step out onto the balcony. Navi lunges towards me, her watery eyes wide with fear.

"Stop them," I pant, gripping my ribs. "Stop them."

She pivots and starts towards them with her sword raised. Her hand is trembling, but she presses forward. Sadal gives me one last dark look before he and Maaz disappear into the shadows of the night. I shout, tears springing to my eyes as Verity disappears with them. Pain tugs at my heart, as if Verity's absence is physically painful to me – as if our hearts were tied together and that knot was suddenly wrenched apart.

Navi falls to her knees beside me as I struggle to my feet. I tear my arm away from her, hissing. "Don't touch me."

She pulls back, gathering herself. We hear a soft whisper and our gazes turn together towards the Bloodbane that was left behind my Maaz and Sadal. The Bloodbane stares disbelievingly towards the balcony, her eyes wide. "They left," she whispers to herself.

"Take her to the dungeons," I command as the door flies open and my soldiers pour in.

Navi leaps to her feet and sheaths her sword. She snatches at the Bloodbane, dragging her from her knees. The soldiers part while Navi forces the Bloodbane out of the room. "Lock the castle down, and get your king a healer," she barks, disappearing down the halls.

The hustling of the castle in chaos falls away as I stare intently at the balcony. The shadows seem alive, coiling chillingly at the edge of the doorway. I wait, hoping that somehow Verity will melt out of the darkness. But she doesn't appear, and the pain in my heart doesn't ease. I bite the inside of my cheek until I draw blood, cursing myself for losing her.

The healers are at my side, asking me questions as they poke and prod me. I ignore them, my gaze never wavering from the doorway. Sadal's arrogant smirk floats through my mind and my hands clench into fists instinctively.

Verity is gone, the curse looming over my head once more. Worse, Sadal's army is coming. I've lost my heart, and now I'll lose my people. I bite back the urge to howl and rage, instead snarling softly to myself.

I will get her back, I vow. Come hell and blood and fire, I will find her. And come darkness and shadow and death, I will kill the Dark God. I taste copper as I swallow my own blood. I will kill him slowly.

CHAPTER 20

VERITY

Pain throbs in my temples and behind my eyes. I groan, rolling to my side slowly. The floor is cold and damp, like wet stone. I cradle my head as I lift my torso and head off the floor. I open my eyes, anticipating pain from bright lights, but the light is dim and gray. Fear coils in my gut as cold pricks at my flesh.

I glance down, studying myself with blurry vision. I'm wearing a black, satin gown with a deep neckline that exposes curves of soft cleavage. My brows furrow with confusion and I trace a finger over the material. Last I remember, I wore a simpler, more modest gown. I don't remember putting this on.

Pain lances through my skull and I inhale sharply, clenching my eyes closed. I bite my lip, suppressing the groans that threaten to escape from my lips. I don't know where I am. If I'm in Altair's castle, then somehow, I've made my way into an unfamiliar wing. But it doesn't feel like Altair's castle. Even the stones ooze a sinister feeling.

I open my eyes again, hissing in pain as I take in my surroundings further. The room is small, half the size of my chamber in Altair's castle. The walls are the same damp stone as the floor, they shimmer as if water trickles down them. There's a window inlaid in the wall, a thin slip of sky with no protection from the elements. Cold wind leaks through it, a howling wind that sends chills down my spine. The wind sounds like demons, their shrieks echoing in the mountains. I shudder.

My eyes rake over the bare chamber. It's empty of everything but bits of stray spread in a corner. My heart quivers as I realize that it reminds me of a cell. I struggle to my feet, holding my head to abate the pressure and pain. I look towards the door, a solid hunk of dark wood, warped and stained. There's a small window with thick bars in the center. Through it, torch light flickers.

I lean against the wall, breathing heavily from the struggle of rising to my feet. The satin gown clings to my legs, wrapped around my ankles. I shiver as another gust of frigid wind breaks through the window and seeps through the stones. I wrap my arms around myself, lips twisted into an anxious frown. I stare around the empty cell, wishing Altair was here.

Where is he? I think, blinking back frightened tears. The last I remember seeing him was when I saw him flying through the sky, before Dain came to my room. Dain. I freeze, eyes widening as I remember. He brought a woman with him, a woman who looked as if she could have been Maaz's sister. A woman with my eyes. My blood turns to ice in my veins and I swallow thickly as I remember the woman striding towards me with her cold gaze. And that's the last thing I remember.

I close my eyes, thinking back to that moment and trying to force my mind to think beyond it. But there's nothing. Just blank, empty space. I was there, and now I'm here. Not remembering is more frightening than this cell or the howling wind. Anything could have happened, and I wouldn't know it. I bite my lip, hoping Altair will stride through the door and announce that he's locked me in a cell to teach me a lesson. At least then I would know where I am.

I peek out the window, standing on the tips of my toes. My eyes barely graze over it. Jagged mountains and snowy peaks stretch across my vision for miles in every direction. The sky is dark, clouded with gray clouds as night falls. Below, shadows writhe in the crags and gullies of the mountains, and the howling of the wind is louder.

I stare at the swirling shadows, squinting to see clearer. I lurch back, a scream lodged in my throat as I spot a sea of yellow eyes glance towards me from the darkness. My back slams into the opposite wall, my chest rising high and fast as I struggle to breathe. This is not Altair's castle. This is the Bloodbane keep – it has to be.

This must have something to do with Dain, I think wildly. He brought the woman with him, a woman that was certainly a Bloodbane witch. But there are no male Bloodbane witches, he must have some other purpose with them. I close my eyes and curse myself for being so stupid these last weeks. I accepted Dain's advances so naively, read the book because I thought he simply wanted to help me. But he didn't want to help me. The only one who wanted to help me was Altair, and I tossed him aside.

"Fucking stupid," I whisper harshly to myself, closing my eyes. "How could I be so fucking stupid?"

Suddenly, I hear a door slam in the hall; the sound echoes down the hall towards me. I lunge for the door, fingers curling around the bars in the small window as I press my face against it. At the end of the hall, towards the torch, I see a red cloak disappear around the corner. I pull away, suspicions confirmed as I lose sight of the witch.

I sigh, eyes roving over my cell as I consider my options. I'm trapped inside the Bloodbane keep, but I don't know how I got here. I don't know if Altair is alive, or if the Bloodbane launched a surprise attack. Fear lances through me as I consider the possibility that Altair might be dead. No, I think fiercely, he can't be. I refuse to believe it.

I want to cry out for him, but I know it wouldn't do any good. I can only hope that he'll come to my rescue now as he did before. I curl in on myself, tears pricking at my eyes as I picture him in my mind; strong, smiling. His hazel eyes flicker through my memories. What I would give to see those eyes once more. What I would give to tell him I'm sorry. Truly sorry.

I think of the Bloodbane book and lash out at the empty room instinctively, imagining that if I could only kick away my memories of it, everything could be fixed. My head snaps towards the door as I hear scraping in the hall, followed by footsteps.

I dart to the corner and press myself into it as the footsteps stop outside the door to my cell. The door creaks open, scraping against the uneven stone floor. I see Maaz first, a cruel smile stretched across her face. She draws her red hood back, exposing her pale blue eyes to the dim light so I can see them gleaming. She saunters into the room, stopping a few feet in front of me.

I open my mouth to speak when someone else follows her, closing the door gently behind them. My eyes widen, lips parting softly as I see Dain move to Maaz's side. He smiles at me, but the smile doesn't reach his eyes. It never did, I realize. His black eyes flicker as a hand snakes around Maaz's waist. She leans into him lovingly, grinning like a cat.

"Dain?" I ask, knowing he isn't the man I thought he was. My voice quivers, but I try to sound strong. "What have you done?"

He chuckles. "No, Verity, what have you done?"

Shame washes over me and I can feel my cheeks heat. "I trusted you," I say weakly.

"I gave you no reason to." He shrugs. He looks amused. "Now, you've single-handedly assured the destruction of Alnembra. Destruction a thousand years in the making."

My heart drops like a stone and my breath catches in my throat. "What?" I choke out.

Dain grins. "My bride and I saw an opportunity and we took it. Alnembra is weak, Altair is weak. And your distance and cruelty has only made it worse. "

Bride? I press myself into the corner even deeper as realization strikes me. Maaz tosses her hair behind her shoulder, eyeing me. "So, you've finally realized. I thought you were smarter than this."

Dain's shadow stretches taller in the unchanged light, the darkness in his eyes expanding until even the whites of his eyes are pitch black. He leers at me, his teeth unnaturally long. My fingers tremble as fear courses through me. Dain is no Fae man. He's a god.

"Sadal," I whisper, eyes wide.

I feel sick to my stomach as I realize that I almost gave myself to the Dark God. I almost chose him over Altair. For one night I did choose him over Altair. I gag, choking back the bile rising in my throat. His bite marks are still on my chest, a terrible reminder of what I've done. Maaz's eyes narrow at my reaction. She lashes out at me, ice cutting across my cheek like needles.

"How dare you?" She hisses, her blue eyes blazing.

Sadal draws her back gently, smiling. He speaks, addressing me, "Someday, Verity, you'll find out that I prefer reluctance to surrender. I love the challenge."

His words make my stomach twist, but I try to school my face. His smile broadens, as if he knows that I don't want to give him the satisfaction of any pleasure – however twisted it may be. Maaz purses her lips, glowering at me. I feel a drop of blood trickle down my cheek from the cut she gave me when she flung her magic at me. I wipe the blood away with the sleeve of my gown.

I eye the pair of them. Where I might have once seen powerful and frightening creatures, I see only my enemies. I feel no fear when I look at them. I only despise myself even more. No matter what, I have to find a way back to Altair. I have to warn him that

Sadal is here. How a Fae could fight a god, I don't know. But I know Altair won't surrender.

"What are those creatures?" I ask, tilting my chin towards the window.

"The horde." Maaz bares her teeth at me in a grin.

"We march on Alnembra," Sadal says, his hand trailing down Maaz's ribs. She shudders with pleasure as he speaks. "We will drench the land in the blood of its people. I'll save Altair for last so he can see the consequences of defying me."

Maaz moans, eyelashes fluttering. "It will be glorious."

Sadal grins and tosses something at my feet. I drop my gaze to it and then recoil. It's the book. "You might get bored in here. There's little to do," Sadal says cruelly.

I stare down at the text, the bits of paper and leather that began everything. I crouch and wrap my thin fingers over the book's binding. It vibrates in my hands, as if awakened. As I rise, my eyes slip towards Sadal and Maaz. They're at the door, leaving. Sadal gives me one last look, winking flirtatiously before the door closes behind them.

The book is warm in my hands as I stare down at it. Anger and fear combine in my chest, flooding through me like a tsunami. I tremble, heat washing over me. I squeeze the book, knuckles turning white as I watch the binding bend to my will. My furious gaze darts up towards the door.

I grin viciously, the book heavy in my hands. If it's a war they want, it's a war I'll give them.

KEEP READING

Grab the Next Book in the series Now!
Seduced by The Fae King
(Mated to The Fae King Book 3)

PREVIEW - SEDUCED BY THE FAE KING

Chapter One

Verity

I wrap the blanket tighter around myself as the frigid chill of cool, mountain air slips into my room. The shutters closed over the window are warped and wet from the day's rain and do little to block the wind. I can hear it howling outside, mingled with the shrieks of the demonic creatures. A shiver trails down my spine that has nothing to do with the chill.

The fireplace is filled with ash and charcoal, smoke curling from the burnt-out embers. I stare into it, at the Bloodbane book I tossed onto the flames. It's unburnt, undamaged from the flames it immediately quenched after I tried to burn it. I tossed it into the fire after reading some of the more gruesome rituals, even worse than the Holy Rite.

My stomach turns as the drawings of the rituals pop into my mind. I've tried to forget them, but some pictures just stay with you. I've spent days since my capture reading the book, teaching myself spells and enchantments that I can use against the Bloodbane. But there was only so much I could read before I made myself sick.

I curl my hands into fists, glaring at the binding of the book. I want the power, but I'm not willing to face the darkness of that power. I feel weak, useless, and guilty. It's my fault that Altair will lose this war against Sadal and the Bloodbane. How could he win against such overwhelming forces of darkness? And I'm unable to help because of my own weakness.

The door handle rattles and my head snaps towards it. I lunge for the book and snatch it from the ash as Sadal slips through the door. His black eyes glide over the ashy book in my hands and he smiles at me.

"Don't like the reading material?" He asks, striding into the room.

I brush the gray embers from the red binding. "You could say that."

I turn towards the hard cot that I've slept on the past few nights and toss the book onto it. For reasons I don't know, Sadal has left the book with me. I suspect he thinks it will tempt as it did before into joining him.

Sadal leans against the fireplace, smirking. His long fingers tap over the dirty stones. "And how do you find your new quarters? Better than a cell, I presume?"

"Not all cells are the same," I whisper.

His eyes narrow. "Ingratitude? From my reluctant bride? What a shock."

"I'm not your bride," I say forcefully, thinking of Altair. "I never will be."

"You think your handsome, Fae prince will save you?" Sadal chuckles. "He'll be dead by the end of the week."

I stare down at my finger, where the engagement ring used to sit. It was taken from me the first night of my arrival here. "What do you want, Sadal?" I ask quietly.

"I came to offer you an invitation." Sadal closes the distance between us. He lifts a finger to my cheek and slowly trails it over my chilled skin. "We move on Alnembra today. Would you like to join me?"

"Do I have a choice?" I stare at him through my eyelashes.

"You do, in fact," Sadal says with a light tone. "Maaz has suggested feeding you to the demons. They're getting awfully hungry – hungry enough to hunt inside our walls from time to time."

I stare at the warped wooden door. That explains the shrill screams of terror that I've heard each night. My eyes snap back to Sadal and I stare at his wicked smile. This man doesn't stop the demons from killing his own people, he might even enjoy it.

"I'll come," I say blandly.

If I stay here in the keep, I'll be useless. The closer I can get to Alnembra, the greater my chances of escape. I might even find a way to sabotage Sadal's army. I picture Altair facing off against Sadal and my heart clenches painfully. Altair could never win against an old god, not without help.

Sadal grins. "Excellent," he purrs. "I can't wait for you to see the glory of my forces."

I don't answer, instead gathering my few belongings into my arms. Instead of the silken dress I wore when I woke up in the keep, I've been given a scratchy woolen shift that keeps me warm. I leave the black gown in the room, there's no need for it anymore. Sadal watches from the door as I collect my things and the book.

"How will we get there?" I ask, following him down the stark halls.

We pass a few Bloodbane witches in their red cloaks. They bow to Sadal, but their eyes are on me. I glare at them as we pass. Sadal leads me into a grand room in the center of the keep, with no windows. Maaz is there, in the center. Her pale blonde hair is coiled into a braid atop her head. She wears a white gown, looking for all the world like a bride despite the red cloak on her shoulders.

She smiles at Sadal, dipping her chin. Her pale blue eyes drift towards me and her smile becomes a scowl. She draws up her hood. "What is she doing here?"

"She'll accompany us to the frontlines." Sadal drops a kiss to Maaz's cheek and I grimace.

"Why?" Maaz asks coldly.

Sadal's black eyes narrow, his lips pressed thin. A chill lances through my chest. He doesn't speak, but his long fingers curl around Maaz's thin shoulder. Her eyes go wide and her face pales. I smirk, watching her curl in on herself in Sadal's intimidating presence.

"Go," he murmurs. "Take your witches and leave. We'll follow."

Maaz nods jerkily and rushes from the room. At the door, she casts a final glance over her shoulder. Her eyes rest on me and I stare morosely at her. The door slams shut, barely missing catching on her red cloak. I feel Sadal behind me, his body emanates power.

"I can't ride a deadwood broom," I say.

"We aren't taking a broom." Sadal's hand sidles over my back and I resist wrenching away from him.

I picture Altair in my mind. I imagine his hazel eyes, his arrogant smirk. When Sadal touches me, I think of Altair. It's the only thing that can stop the panic and disgust that wells inside me when Sadal touches me.

Suddenly, Sadal loops a strong arm around my waist and pulls me into his chest. I yelp, trying to pull away but he holds me fast. Sadal's face is peaceful, as if unbothered by my struggle. He smiles broadly down at me, too wide for his face.

"Lanuae praesens," Sadal murmurs.

Suddenly, my vision goes black and the ground beneath my feet tips away from me. I scream breathlessly as Sadal's grip tightens around me. Air whooshes around me, loud in my ears. An instant later, bright white light blinds me, and I collapse to the earth. Sweat drips down my forehead and my arms shake.

Panting, I stare down at the rocky, gray earth beneath me. Puffs of dust prick at my eyes as I breathe. As my eyes adjust, I can make out distant green fields below the gray slopes of the mountain. I lift myself to my knees and stare out at my surroundings.

Sadal has brought me to the slopes of the mountains near Alnembra's border. I can't see the palace or the sea in the distance, which sets my heart at ease. I twist and stare at Sadal. The wind whips his black jacket behind him as he smiles down at me. A chill runs down my spine. He stretches out his hand just as I hear a massive bellow bounce off of the mountains. The demons.

I scramble to my feet, ignoring his hand, and rush to the edge of the steep slope. My stomach drops as I take in the sight. Below, stretching from the barren slopes of the mountain to the first grove of trees in Alnembra, is a massive, black horde. The shadows writhe and twist as the demons jostle in their ranks. There are no flags to signify which units are camped where, no tents for the demons to sleep in. They're beasts; foul and vicious.

My breath is lodged in my throat as I listen to their screams. I hadn't noticed so many of the demons marching away from the keep since my capture. Here, there are tens of thousands. Sadal joins me, his shoulders straight and proud.

"Magnificent, isn't it?" He muses. "Imagine the carnage when we strike Altair's forces."

And I do.

I imagine red blood soaking the earth, spilling into the fae rivers and streams. I imagine Fae bodies piling up as the demons scramble over them to kill more. I imagine Altair, falling in battle, overwhelmed by monsters.

My hands tremble and I stuff them into the folds of my skirt to hide it from Sadal. He turns away, drawing me from the sight of his destructive forces. On another plateau, I see an assembly of tents, likely the Bloodbane forces. Above it, I see red cloaks swirling in the sky.

"Come, love," Sadal says, taking my hand. "You must be tired; we can rest in our tent."

My eyes widen at his words and I stare towards the grand tent covered in luxurious fabrics in the center of camp. Our tent. My stomach twists and I swallow the bile rising in my throat. I glance over my shoulder, towards Alnembra. I imagine I see Altair's beastly form soaring through the skies, but I know it's only a cloud.

I slip into the darkness of the tent, ice in my veins.

Want to keep reading?
Grab Your Copy Now!

ABOUT THE AUTHOR

Bailey Dark is obsessed with all things dark, hot, and supernatural. From Fae to Aliens, her heroes are thoroughly alpha and pure raw masculinity. When she's not writing (which is hardly ever) she's busy watching every movie in the marvel universe, or binging supernatural on her couch. So come along, and enter her dark world. . . .

baileydarkauthor.com

ALSO BY BAILEY DARK

Mated to The Fae King

(Completed Series - Fantasy Romance)

Also Available in Audio!

1. Stolen by The Fae King

2. Destined for The Fae King

3. Seduced by The Fae King

4. Claimed by The Fae King

5. Forever with The Fae King

Captive of Shadows

(Completed Series - Fantasy Romance)

Also Available in Audio!

1. Promised to The Shadow King

2. Trial for The Shadow King

3. Awakened by The Shadow King

4. Battle for The Shadow King

5. Eternity with The Shadow King

Warlords of Farian

(Completed Series - SciFi Romance)

1. The Beast King's Bride

2. Taken by The Alpha Warlord

3. The Commander's Virgin Queen

4. The Barbarian's Captive

5. Chosen by The Berserker

Warlords of Farian The Complete Boxed Set

Moon Cursed

(Current Series - Paranormal Romance)

Also Available in Audio!

1. Her Shifter King

2. Her Shifter Mate

3 -TBA

The Labyrinth Curse

(Current Series - Fantasy Romance)

Coming Soon in Audio!

1. The Twisted King

2. Coming Soon!

3. TBA

SUBSCRIBE & CLAIM YOUR FREE BOOK!

Want to know all the latest updates?
Join My Newsletter
Let me do the work for you! I'll email you anytime I have a new release (or something awesome to share!)

PLUS GET A FREE BOOK FOR JOINING!

www.ingramcontent.com/pod-product-compliance
Lightning Source LLC
Chambersburg PA
CBHW031312160726
47993CB00001B/392